MW01502876

Finding Forever
In Romance

A Fall Into Romance Novella

Melanie D. Snitker

Finding Forever in Romance
A Fall Into Romance Novella
© 2017 Melanie D. Snitker

Published by
Dallionz Media, LLC
P.O. Box 6821
Abilene, TX 79608

Cover: Blue Valley Author Services

For permission requests, please contact the author at the e-mail below or through her website.

Melanie D. Snitker
melaniedsnitker@gmail.com
www.melaniedsnitker.com

This is a work of fiction. Names, characters, businesses, places, events, and incidents either are the products of the author's imagination or used in a fictitious manner. Any resemblance to actual persons, living or dead, or actual events is purely coincidental.

ISBN-10: 1979015228
ISBN-13: 978-1979015226

In memory of my grandpa, Howard Shults.
With love always from your Number One.

Chapter One

A blurry mass of fur raced past Brent toward the main building of the Finding Forever Animal Rescue. Brent pinned the black leash to the ground with his foot before it got out of reach. Steeling himself, he waited for the Great Dane to hit the end of his dash for freedom. The dog jerked to a stop and nearly took Brent's foot right out from under him. Once he regained his balance, Brent reached down for the leash and held tight.

Stacie Rosenthal, a high school student who volunteered at Finding Forever whenever she could, came running toward them from the building that housed the larger kennels. Hair escaped her ponytail every which way. The girl couldn't be more than five foot two. Why on earth was she walking this miniature horse? The dog stood calmly as if he had all the time in the world.

Stacie stared at the canine with wide eyes. "I'm sorry, Mr. Todd. I didn't know he'd run from me. Does he usually do that?"

"Who? Costello, here?" He didn't even have to lean down to give the dog a hearty pat on the rump. "Every time. Why don't I take him back, and we'll let Walt walk him?"

There was no missing the relief on the teen's face as she nodded. Brent was always thankful for every volunteer at the shelter. He couldn't keep the place running without them. But it was best to leave some of the larger guests to those who could better handle their—um—rambunctious nature.

They found Walt in the back. A senior in college, he'd worked for the shelter over the last year and a half. Walt worked several hours a day unless he had an exam coming up. He showed a true love for animals and was one of only two paid employees at Finding Forever. That included Brent himself, who owned and ran it. Walt quickly agreed to take Costello for a walk, and the pair disappeared.

Stacie attempted to smooth her hair back into place, but the strands refused to be tamed. "I sure hope Costello finds a family soon."

"Yeah, me, too." The dog had lived at the animal shelter for over six months now. He ate a ton of food and was generally a troublemaker. But that was only because he was a year-and-a-half old puppy wrapped in the body of a small horse. He'd make a great family dog. But when people came in search of a new furry member of the family, Costello's size and exuberance put them off.

The annual town festival benefiting the shelter usually brought in the money needed to keep it running for the rest of the year. The festival was just over three weeks away. Brent hoped Costello would be one of the many animals placed in a new home.

Brent noted the time on his phone before slipping it into one of the cargo pockets of his pants. "You'd better finish up, Stacie. It's almost four-thirty, and your mom will be expecting you home soon. Are all the animals fed for the evening?"

"Every last one." Stacie gave a nod. "I even checked on Kip and her kittens. I sure wish my mom would let me take one home."

"Maybe if you bring her by the adoption station at the festival, she'll see them and won't be able to resist." He smiled at her.

Stacie grinned back. "I seriously doubt it, but it's worth a try. Thanks, Mr. Todd. See you next week!"

"Bye, Stacie."

He watched her leave. She disappeared followed by the smile on his face. Truthfully, he wasn't sure the proceeds from this year's festival would be enough. Most years, he barely squeaked by as it was. He hadn't told Walt yet, but he was worried about paying the kid's wages after the end of the year.

Brent wandered to the front room of the farmhouse he'd turned into the rescue center. The place was a dream come true. He had close to seventy animals in his care, including abandoned livestock, that relied on him to find them homes. He didn't want to surrender any of them to animal control. But if he couldn't raise more money or find more help…

He swallowed his apprehension and pushed the thought aside. One way or another, he'd figure something out. He had to.

At a quarter to five, Walt said goodbye for the day. Brent did his usual walk-through, checking to make sure all the animals were taken care of and secure. Then he grabbed the stack of flyers off the counter, switched the sign to closed on the front door, and locked up.

If he hurried, he could deliver at least some of the flyers around town before most of the businesses closed for the day.

It was Monday in the little town of Romance, Oregon. With a population of around thirty thousand, Brent thought it was just the right size. It was big enough to have many of the amenities most people wanted in a town, yet still maintain a small-town atmosphere. It was true going to the store usually resulted in seeing at least two people he knew. Every time. The thought tugged one corner of his mouth upward. He couldn't imagine living anywhere else in the world.

Residents raced to get home for the evening. To most of them, this was the first day of the work week. Not that it really mattered to Brent. For him, work at Finding Forever never truly ended, and the weekends only got busier with fewer volunteers helping.

Low clouds hovered, threatening the forecasted rain. Not unusual for Romance in September. Or any other time of the year, for that matter. The lush grass, green trees, and moss mottling the concrete steps and fences spoke of the frequent precipitation.

Brent made several stops, handing out flyers for store owners to put up in their establishments. Everyone expressed their excitement at the upcoming fifth annual festival and jumped at the chance to help.

At almost five-thirty, he pulled into the little parking lot next to the Romance Family Skating Rink. The lot was nearly empty, which meant the open roller skate was over, and most of the kids had gone home.

The roller rink had been a fixture of the town for decades and was refurbished several years ago. It was a great place for families to spend time together. The local roller hockey club met and played there as well. Brent's friend Jim had helped organize the club for years. Jim also coached one of the teams during the tournaments, and Brent used to help him. Only now did he realize it'd been at least a year since the last time he'd made the effort.

He stepped out of his car, and the first raindrop landed on the tip of his ear. Tucking the flyers under his windbreaker, he increased his pace to the front door and pulled it open.

The smell of rubber, dirty socks, and wax clashed as warm air engulfed him when he entered. He remembered roller skating when he was a kid and it'd smelled exactly like this. The memories brought a smile to his face.

No one was at the admittance window. Sounds of laughter filtered through the door leading inside. He pulled that open and spotted two people out on the rink.

A flash of red hair went by. Nicole Crawford. A single mom, she'd managed the roller rink and was nearly always there when he used to help coach. Her son Tony had practically grown up playing the sport.

The last time Brent saw her, Nicole's hair reached her waist. It was one of many features he'd always admired. He'd often watched her and Jim joke back and forth and assumed they would end up together one day. Or at least that was the excuse he made when rejecting all thoughts of asking Nicole out.

Then Jim married Cassandra, his high school sweetheart. That's about the time when things picked up at the shelter. Since then, Brent barely got away from the place. He certainly didn't have the time necessary to devote to dating someone like Nicole. So he'd avoided going to the rink this past year.

Nicole must have cut her hair. It swished just below her shoulder blades as the lights above reflected off the dark crimson tresses. Strands clung to her flushed cheeks, and her bright blue eyes glittered as she kept her gaze on Tony.

They both gripped hockey sticks as they came around one goal and skated toward the other end of the rink. Tony moved the puck back and forth with ease before letting it sail to Nicole. With a fluid motion, she brought her stick back and accepted the pass.

Brent headed to the benches along one side and took a seat to watch the exchange. Tony had to be what? Twelve now? He was nearly as tall as his mom and full of energy. But if Brent remembered right, Nicole was a spitfire and could hold her own.

The pair crossed the center line and picked up speed. As they neared the other goal, Nicole passed the puck to Tony. He accepted it and quickly hit it right into the goal with a clang that echoed through the rink. His face spread into a grin. He circled the goal, came back around, and gave his mom a high five.

Mother and son glided on inline skates to the small door that allowed them to exit. That's when they spotted Brent.

Tony lifted a hand in greeting. "Hey, Mr. Todd! We haven't seen you in a while." The boy's red t-shirt with the name of his hockey team, the Wildcats, had rings of sweat around the collar and under the arms. Tony always had been a hard worker, and he'd told

Brent more than once that roller hockey was his favorite thing.

"Hi, Tony." Brent stuck a hand out and shook the pre-teen's hand. "I know, it's been too long. I've missed watching you all play."

Tony collapsed onto the bleacher and bent to untie his skates. "Even though you aren't coaching anymore, you should come by and watch. We have a game this Saturday."

"I'll do that one of these weekends." Brent's attention turned to Nicole. They were nearly the same height while she wore her skates. He took in her blue eyes and the hair that framed her delicate face. A small smattering of freckles covered her nose and upper cheeks. Altogether, it gave her a youthful appearance. He'd always thought her pretty. But now, when her cheeks were red from playing hockey with her son…

"Hi, Brent. What brings you here?"

What? Oh, right.

He lifted the flyers he'd nearly forgotten about. "I was wondering if you could display a couple of these for the festival. It's only a few weeks away, and I'd like to get solid participants soon. I'm hoping we can beat last year's record on the number of booths present."

Nicole rocked back and forth on her skates and reached for one of the flyers. She scanned it and nodded. "Of course. I'll put one out front and another in the break room." She took the small stack he handed her and tucked them under one arm. "You're looking for volunteers, too?"

He wasn't surprised she'd noticed that smaller print near the bottom of the flyer. Nicole always was one for catching the details. He usually kept festival business to just that — anything to do with the festival.

But he was getting desperate for help at the shelter and had mentioned something about it on the flyers. If someone didn't want to have a booth at the festival, perhaps they'd be willing to volunteer a couple hours a week. At least Brent could only hope. He shrugged. "I've been running low on help lately."

Tony stood up, skates under one arm. "Mom, is it okay if I go grab a snack before I help clean up?"

"Sure. Thanks, Tony." Nicole watched her son head to the break room on the other end of the building. She turned her attention back to Brent, her brows drawn together in concern. "I don't recall you ever asking for help for the shelter. Is everything okay?"

Brent knew he should've stuck to festival business. He ought to tell her all was well. But he hesitated too long, and it seemed to be the reaction Nicole needed.

She tipped her head toward the front. "Let me go lock up, and then you can tell me what's going on."

~

Nicole made sure the front door was secure before skating her way to the break room. Brent followed close behind. Tony passed them on the way out, a bag of chips in one hand. Nicole shook her head, marveling at his unending energy. Tony rarely stayed in one place for long. He also never complained about helping her clean the rink at the end of the day. She couldn't ask for a more thoughtful son.

When she and Brent got inside, she sat down and removed the inline skates from her feet. "Would you like a pop?"

"Sure."

"You still drink Dr Pepper?"

Brent's brown eyes widened as if he were surprised she remembered. But there were many times when he'd drop by, and he and Jim would chat for a while or watch the teams play. Brent often had a Dr Pepper in his hands.

She retrieved a glass bottle from the fridge in the corner and got herself an IBC root beer. He flashed her one of his killer grins. Oh, and that dimple! Her pulse picked up speed just like it used to, as if only hours or days had passed instead of nearly a year. Apparently, not swinging by the rink hadn't been a big deal for him. But she'd missed it a lot.

They sat down at one of the picnic-style tables. Brent withdrew a multi-tool from his pocket and removed the bottlecap from his pop. He reached for hers and did the same before handing it back.

"Thanks." Nicole smiled at him and took a sip. She willed her thumping heart to calm down. They'd been friends back when he used to frequent the rink. Nothing had changed. She had a son to raise on her own, and the last thing she needed was an emotional distraction. She'd told herself that very same thing back then, too. "So, what's going on with the shelter?"

Brent took a long drink before setting the pop bottle down. He shrugged. "Nothing I won't find a solution for." But when Nicole raised an eyebrow at him, he kept talking. "Long story short, I've got more animals in the rescue center than ever before, and a record low on the number of volunteers." He put a hand on the back of his neck.

"What happened to them? I thought you usually had a surplus of volunteers." Nicole rotated the base of her pop bottle on the table, the condensation creating wet rings.

"I did for several years. A lot of the kids graduated and went off to college. Or their families moved. I can't seem to get a renewed interest. There are several repairs I should do plus a serious need to expand. And I'm struggling with funds to cover even one of those."

The worried expression on Brent's face elicited a similar reaction in her. "Are there more animals coming in now? Or fewer people adopting?"

"Honestly? A little of both. I often drove some of the dogs or exotic critters to a shelter in Portland, but now that's over capacity too. I don't have a lot of options right now."

Having a place for homeless animals was a dream Brent had had since he was a child. He did a lot of good for the community. Nicole sure hated the thought of the shelter closing. There'd be no place for the animals to go outside of animal control, and they weren't nearly as dedicated to helping them find new homes as Brent was.

"I'm glad you put the need for volunteers at the bottom of the flyers. Hopefully it'll drum up interest."

"I hope so." But Brent didn't appear convinced. He took another drink. "If things don't improve soon, I'm not sure I'll be able to keep the shelter open for another year." He clenched his teeth.

Nicole knew how hard it was to keep going against all odds. She'd been naïve when she'd married her high school sweetheart at the tender age of nineteen. She became pregnant later that year and thought everything was perfect. Until Stephen told her out of the blue he wanted a divorce. When she tried to figure out what happened, he claimed she made the relationship too difficult and walked out on both her and Tony. It wasn't because of her. Or Tony. But sometimes it was hard to keep that doubt from creeping in.

It'd been a harsh introduction to how cruel reality could be. And she'd been going against the odds, raising her son on her own, ever since.

When Tony was much younger, Nicole had thought she could have a second chance at finding love. She made the mistake of allowing herself to venture into relationships that only left her hurt and Tony confused. When the last guy walked away leaving six-year-old Tony devastated, she promised herself she wouldn't do that to him again.

Funds may have been limited, but she and Tony were happy and their life was stable. Only now, sitting across from Brent, did Nicole give her isolation any consideration. Still, being lonely was a small price to pay to keep Tony from experiencing the hurt previous relationships had dealt.

It sounded like Brent was all on his own when it came to keeping the shelter open. Her heart went out to him. Nicole had experience trying to keep things together even when everything was falling apart around her.

"I think the last time you came by the skating rink was a year ago."

Brent shrugged. "If so, that's sad I only drop by when I want you to post something up on your message board, isn't it?" He put his hand on the back of his neck again before finishing his pop. "With everything going on, I guess I haven't been making much time for socializing."

Nicole understood. But while Brent might be Jim's friend, Nicole had always enjoyed visiting with him, too. She'd missed seeing him this last year. Was it terrible that she wished he'd come to games again so she could run into him more often?

Brent set the empty bottle down on the table. "What about you? Are you and Tony doing okay?"

Nicole nodded. "We're fine." Except that she wasn't sure how true that was, either. She was lonely, exhausted, and wedged in a rut. She'd been working here at the skating rink for years, barely scraping by, and couldn't see the end of it. But what would be the point of telling him that?

Brent didn't look like he believed her, but he let it go. He stood from the table, put his bottle in a recycling bin, and jabbed a thumb toward the front of the rink. "I'd better get going. Thanks for the Dr Pepper. It was good to see you, Nicole."

She followed suit. "You, too. I'll be hoping you get a lot of calls in the next week from people wanting to help out at the shelter."

"I appreciate it."

Nicole followed him to the door. "Hey, don't be a stranger."

He rewarded her with a dimpled grin and waved a farewell. After pulling his hood over his head, he ducked and made a beeline for his vehicle. A steady rain was falling now with an accompanying chill in the air. She rubbed her upper arms to warm herself back up again.

The sound of Tony walking up behind her made her turn around.

"I think we're ready to go." He scrutinized the weather. "Should we wait for a few minutes for it to clear up?"

Nicole shook her head. "I checked the weather, and it might be like this for a while. May as well go home." She reached over and ruffled his hair. The very idea that he was no longer her little boy but a young man threatened tears. When had that happened? She sniffed, forcing her emotions into check.

"What was Mr. Todd doing here?"

"He brought flyers to put up for the festival."

Tony said nothing, but that all-too-familiar sparkle came into his eyes.

Nicole put her hands on her hips. "What?"

"I wish you'd let me get a dog this year. You know I'd take good care of it. Seriously, Mom." Those brown eyes, much like Stephen's, bore right into her heart.

There was no doubt he'd take care of a pet. Tony was way more reliable and self-sufficient than a kid his age ought to be. But the thought of dealing with a puppy right now pushed her never-ending exhaustion into overdrive.

Brent's words about how there were fewer animals being adopted came to mind. Maybe, if they adopted a young, adult dog, the work would be easier. The idea had merit. She reached out and squeezed his shoulder. "You ready to make a run for it?"

"You bet."

They slipped their jackets on, pulled the hoods up over their heads, and exited the building.

If Nicole still liked the idea brewing in her head tomorrow, she'd see what Tony thought. Although, if

13

she knew her son, they'd be paying a visit to Brent at Finding Forever real soon.

Chapter Two

After leaving the skating rink, Brent had a hard time getting Nicole out of his head. He'd regretted not escaping the rescue center more and spending time with his friends over the last year.

It seemed like something was going on with Nicole. Whatever it was, she clearly hadn't wanted to talk about it. And he certainly didn't feel comfortable pushing her for information.

Was everything okay with her job? Was she having any issues with Tony?

He spent the evening searching for a good excuse to go back and check on her. Everything he came up with sounded lame.

He was surprised and pleased to see Nicole walk in with her son later the next morning. While the rain had eased up a little since yesterday, both still had to shake water off their jackets as they stepped inside the shelter.

Brent walked around the desk area he'd set up in what used to be the farmhouse's living room. "Good morning. What brings the two of you here?"

Tony dried his hands off on his pants and took in the large pictures of pets on the walls. "Hey, Mr. Todd." He seemed interested in everything, his gaze stopping at one poster showing different breeds of dogs.

Nicole used both hands to smooth her hair into place. Little droplets of rain made the red strands shine like sun on a field of red roses. "Tony has wanted a dog for years. He's given me a pretty convincing argument for why we should get one. He doesn't remember the last time we had a pet. I thought it might be a good idea for him to see what caring for one would be like. And since you need volunteers…"

Tony grinned as if someone had handed him a stack of money. "Mom says we should volunteer until the festival, and then I can pick out a dog."

Brent checked the clock. It was almost ten. "Is school out today?"

"We homeschool." Nicole slipped her hands into the pockets of her dark jeans. "We got a chunk of work done before we came over. We can finish the rest this afternoon before the rink opens. That's the beauty of overseeing our own schedule." She winked at Tony.

Brent nodded. He'd known they homeschooled but had forgotten. Yet more evidence showing how sequestered he'd been out here at the shelter. He should've been keeping better track of how things were going for his friends, and that included Nicole.

A larger number of his volunteers could work in the afternoons. To have someone else help in the morning hours would be great. When they'd first come in, Nicole appeared interested and happy. Now she seemed nervous as she nibbled on her bottom lip. Brent quickly assured her he'd love their help. "How about a tour first?"

The duo agreed. A bell on the door would let him know if someone else came in. He led the way around the central counter and down one hallway. "There are three rooms this way: Two for the cats and the other contains the exotics."

"Exotics?" Tony's brows rose. "Like bobcats or something?"

Brent chuckled. "No, that includes anything that's not a dog, a cat, or livestock. I don't normally have a lot of animals that fall under that category. But today I've got quite a few including a pair of guinea pigs, a rabbit, a cage full of ferrets, and a flying squirrel that came in a few days ago. That's been a learning experience, let me tell you."

Nicole could only imagine. She smiled at the pile of ferrets snoozing in a hammock in the corner of their cage. She couldn't even tell how many there were or where one animal began and the other ended. A little orange, white, and brown face lifted, eyes blinking against the light, before the little guy went back to sleep again.

It was the flying squirrel that Tony was focused on. His gaze swung to his mom's, and Nicole immediately shook her head. "Don't even think about it."

Tony gave a good-natured roll of his eyes but kept a smile in place. "This used to be a farmhouse, right? Why did you turn it into a shelter?"

Brent paused in the hallway as meows floated out to meet them. "I grew up in this neighborhood, just down the street. When I was a kid, I loved all animals. I don't know how many of them I took home, begging my parents to let me keep them." He laughed at the memories. Even though his parents limited him on the number of animals he could keep as pets, they always felt sympathetic to his need to find homes for the rest. "Howard Rice used to own this house. He was an older gentleman who loved to sit on the front porch and carve almost anything out of wood with his pocket knife. Every time I'd pass by, he'd say hello. And every time he saw me with another animal, he'd laugh and ask if it was a new addition to my zoo."

Brent shook his head, unable to keep the smile off his face. Back then, old Mr. Rice was one of the friendliest people on the block.

"After a while, he'd see me coming with an animal, and he'd meet me out front. Usually with leftovers to share. Once, he even found a kitten in his backyard and gave it to me because he knew I'd find it a good home."

Nicole brushed some hair behind her right ear. "He sounds like a great guy."

"Yeah, he was. By the time I graduated from high school, he was like another grandfather to me." Brent reached into a front pocket and pulled out the small carved figure of a German shepherd. "He gave me this, and I've kept it ever since."

Tony ran a finger over the head of the figurine. "Cool!"

Brent noted that Nicole seemed to be as interested in his story as Tony. "Even after I graduated high school, I was determined to form a rescue group. When I was twenty-one, Mr. Rice died. A lawyer showed up one day and announced Mr. Rice had left this house to me. The only stipulation was that I keep on rescuing animals and doing what I loved." Brent shrugged. "I've lived here and tried to do that ever since. I stay upstairs, but the bottom floor is dedicated to the animals."

Nicole put a hand to her lips and smiled, her eyes moist. "That's amazing. What a blessing Mr. Rice was."

"I couldn't agree more." Brent motioned for them to precede him into the nearest room that housed the exotic animals he'd mentioned. The black and white dwarf bunny stuck its nose out of the cage allowing Nicole to pet it. After that, they checked out both rooms dedicated to the cats. Kip meowed and her kittens sat up to peer through the crate door at them. The cacophony of mews and yowls had Tony grinning as he stuck a finger through cages and petted as many cats as he could.

Nicole followed Brent as he led them out to the main room again. "How long does it usually take to find homes for the animals? On average?"

"It depends. Some stay for a day or two. Others are here for months." A hoarse meow sounded from the counter as a black cat jumped onto it. "This is Stormy. She was a guest here for four months. But she has such a great personality and was so stubborn, I decided she deserved to be my mascot."

Tony reached a hand out, and Stormy had no problems rubbing up against it, her purr-box whirring into full-speed. Nicole ran the knuckles of one hand over the top of Stormy's head. "She's a sweetheart."

"That she is. Most of the time. Unless you tell her no, and then she can be vindictive. I have no plants on this counter because she'll knock them off during one of her hissy fits." Brent laughed.

Nicole joined him, her soft voice filling the room.

Brent led them down the other hall. "We keep all the larger breeds in the kennels out back. But I don't have enough of those, and they aren't nearly as climate controlled as I'd like. So, the toy breeds stay here along with any who have special needs."

Barks called to them as they entered one of the two rooms. He introduced them to a variety of dogs, including Chihuahuas, a dachshund, a silky, and a few more. He stopped at a larger kennel that housed a basset hound. "This older fella can't handle the colder temperatures outside." He reached a hand through the kennel. The poor guy gazed up at him with sad eyes before running a tongue across Brent's hand. "Toby's owner died, and he had nowhere else to go."

"I don't know how you do this." Nicole's voice was quiet, and there was no missing the sadness in it. "It's heartbreaking."

"It is." Brent knew that firsthand. "But we give them a chance to find their forever families here, and they'd have much less of a chance over with animal control. Especially guys like Toby. It's hard, but at least he's warm, fed, and safe."

~

Nicole couldn't take her eyes off Toby. The sweet old guy kept wagging his tail as Brent patted him. It'd be difficult to find an older dog like this a home. She could tell the next few weeks of volunteering would be difficult ones when she had to see this many animals waiting for families to adopt them.

"You okay?"

Brent's voice came from near Nicole's right shoulder, and she startled. He was standing close enough for her to smell his aftershave. She hazarded a glance at her son before nodding. "Yeah. I just feel for the poor dog."

"I know. But you guys volunteering will help a lot. Even an hour a week makes a huge difference."

Was it crazy that Nicole was already trying to figure out how many hours they could volunteer and still get school done before opening the rink in the afternoon?

"Alright, this last room down here is the one our veterinarians use. Robert Foster or his wife, Allie, volunteer every Friday to see how we're doing." Brent switched on the light to reveal a room set up with a table, two chairs, and cabinets along one wall. "Between this room and their mobile vet clinic, they can spay and neuter any animals that need it, and tend to any that are sick."

Nicole looked around the room. "Rob's my friend Audrey's brother. I've met him a few times and hear a lot of great things about their Happy Paws Animal Hospital. He and Allie seem nice. That's great they come here every week. Much easier than trying to get all these animals into their clinic."

Nicole and Tony followed Brent through the house into the backyard and to the large, red building not far away. Their jackets kept the mist in the air off their clothes.

The barks and howls beckoned them inside. As soon as they entered, happy animals greeted them with wagging tails, all watching the newcomers.

"We've got larger dogs out here. Ranging from a Border Collie mix up to our giant Great Dane and that guy over there."

The sheer volume of barks kept Nicole's ears ringing. She took in the two large dogs and frowned. "Are they all friendly?"

Brent turned to study her, his expression serious. "Absolutely. Rob and Allie check them all to ensure they are in good health. I try to work with each of them. Not all the dogs are great with cats or what have you, but they are friendly. I've gotten some animals that are not, and I send them to a shelter up near Portland. Or I've sometimes had to take them over to animal control. But I try to avoid that when I can."

Nicole was glad to hear it. Especially after observing the Great Dane and the other dog that seemed to be at least part bull mastiff. The thought of her son being around an unfriendly dog as large as either of them only increased her anxiety.

Brent put a hand on her shoulder. "Tony will only be involved with the animals you want him to manage. And you can be right there with him if you prefer."

Apparently, she hadn't been hiding her worries as well as she'd thought. She nodded, meeting his gaze. His brown eyes were awash with concern, as though he were trying to get a glimpse into why she hesitated. He seemed to either get the information he wanted, or chose to put aside his curiosities.

"These are indoor/outdoor kennels which makes cleaning up easier and gives the dogs more room to roam. I want another building like this. One that's climate controlled where we can house the smaller dogs. They would be happier."

Tony had his hand against one kennel, happily accepting the wet kisses from a terrier mix. "This was an old farm. Do you take farm animals?"

"We do. I usually send them over to Blayne Grundy at the Rockin' G Ranch. He's better equipped to handle livestock, and his place is only about ten miles out of town. We do have a small barn and corral on the other side of the property plus four acres of fenced pasture. I can keep some livestock here for a short while. We almost always have chickens."

He motioned for them to follow him again back to the main house. "I'm the only one here for another couple of hours, and I try to stay in the house in case someone comes by to adopt an animal."

Nicole took in the chipping paint that made up the house's siding and the unkept bushes along the walkways. It was clear almost all the money that came into Finding Forever Animal Rescue went directly to the animals. With the number of pets he cared for, no wonder he needed more volunteers.

Once they got back inside, Tony asked if he could go watch the dogs. Nicole agreed that he could and then turned to talk to Brent. "Do you have particular hours you could use help the most?"

Stormy jumped onto the counter again and immediately rubbed her cheek along Nicole's arm. Nicole chuckled as she stroked the cat's silky fur. "I can see why you couldn't resist keeping her."

Brent grinned, revealing a small dimple in his right cheek. "It's hard not to keep them all." He pulled out his phone and opened the calendar. "Honestly, I can use the most help either late morning or early afternoon. Either time, Tony would be a huge help walking the dogs and playing with them for a while."

Nicole nodded, calculating time and how much Tony needed to get his schoolwork done. "If we can bring a lunch, what about ten to one Tuesday, Wednesday, and Thursday?"

Brent's eyes widened.

Was that not enough? Too much? She probably should've started with one day a week, right?

"If you're certain. You can always cut back the hours if you decide it's too much."

"We'll keep that in mind. But yes, I'm certain. I want Tony to know what it takes to have a pet before we get one ourselves."

Brent picked up Stormy and set her on the floor. "Always a good idea. Do you want to start tomorrow, or wait until next week?"

"Tomorrow sounds great. Anything we need to bring?"

Brent thought a moment. "Like you said, bring a lunch. And wear clothes you don't care about getting dirty."

Nicole nodded again. "That sounds good. In that case, I'll go see if I can convince Tony to leave the animals for now, and we'll see you tomorrow."

He smiled again, and Nicole's heart skipped a beat. Unwilling to examine why she was reacting this way, they found Tony and filled him in on their volunteer schedule and grinned when her son's eyes gleamed.

"I can't wait. Thanks, Mr. Todd."

Brent stuck a hand out and shook Tony's before escorting them to the main door. "I appreciate your time, both of you."

Nicole waved behind her as they made their way back to the car. The whole drive home, Tony didn't stop talking about the animals he'd seen and how much he couldn't wait for the next day.

Nicole couldn't get a word in edgewise. She had to admit she was looking forward to it, too. But her nerves were kicking into high gear. What was up with her reaction toward Brent? She used to have what she considered a crush on him. But surely that had disappeared in the year she hadn't seen him. Maybe it was the lack of sleep last night.

Or maybe it was because she'd been lamenting to herself about feeling lonely lately. Whatever it was, it didn't matter. She was a single mom of an almost teen boy. And the last thing she wanted was for her or Tony to get close to someone, only to have him walk away. Tony may not remember Stephen leaving, but Nicole certainly did.

Brent was a friend she'd known for years, and that was how it would stay.

Chapter Three

Brent appreciated the fact Tony caught on quickly. Once Brent showed him how to leash and walk the smaller dogs, the boy went right to work. Brent wasn't sure who enjoyed the interactions more: Tony or the dogs.

Every day, Brent tried to make sure the indoor dogs got outside three times. Sometimes more, if he could swing it. But the trips were usually much shorter than he would have liked. Tony took them outside, played ball or ran with them for fifteen minutes, and brought the contented dogs back in.

Tony was all smiles, too. And that smile was a mirror image of Nicole's. There was no doubt they were mother and son. The rest of Tony's features, however, must take after his dad. Brent remembered hearing someone talk at the skating rink a few years ago about how the guy had walked out on his family, but that was all he knew. Nicole certainly never talked about it. Brent couldn't fathom leaving like that and wouldn't mind meeting the guy long enough to give him a good right cross.

When Nicole asked what she should do, Brent suggested feeding and watering the cats.

"Do you want me to clean their litter boxes, too?"

Brent hesitated to assign the unpleasant chore on the first day. But it was clear by her expression the offer was sincere. He nodded. "If you're sure you don't mind. Here, let me show you where everything is."

Nicole didn't hesitate to get started. Brent followed her in, carrying a large bag of cat litter. Nicole seemed to be a natural with the animals. She talked softly to the cat she was working with while cleaning the litter box, filling up the food and water bowls, and even giving the cat some attention. A few minutes later, he returned with a new bag of cat food. This time, Nicole was loving on the little calico someone brought in last week.

The big shock was that the cat was purring as she rubbed the top of her head against the bottom of Nicole's chin. And Nicole indulged the cat with scratches behind her ears and along her neck.

"You're such a pretty kitty. I wonder where you came from. How anyone can see you and not want to take you home is beyond me."

Brent cleared his throat. "You're the first person who's been able to hold her in the week she's been here. She hides in the back of her crate whenever someone comes in to look for a cat. No one gives her a second glance when other cats are vying for attention."

Nicole frowned and regarded the cat who had curled up in her lap. "That's just sad. I'll bet if she'd act friendly at all, someone would adopt her in a heartbeat."

"Sometimes it takes the animals a while to come out of their shell. I'm sure you're right, and hopefully she'll find a home soon."

Nicole continued to pet the cat for several moments before coaxing her into the kennel again. The calico meowed once and curled up in the back. She was nearly invisible except for the gold eyes that seemed to glow in the dark.

"Well, that'll break your heart."

Brent nodded but said nothing. He didn't blame Nicole if she decided volunteering there wasn't for her. Although he selfishly hoped she'd continue. Partly because he needed help, but also because he found he enjoyed her company.

She brushed cat hair off her clothing. "You mentioned Stormy was the center's mascot. How have you managed to not adopt a dozen more animals yourself?"

It wasn't the first time someone had voiced the same question. He leaned against a shelf holding some supplies. "It's not because I don't want to." He gestured around the room. "But for every pet I'd adopt, I'd feel guilty I left a dozen more down here without a permanent home. Instead of having to make that choice, I try to care for them all as best I can." Did she think his decision made him weak? Uncaring? He watched her face as she considered his words.

"That's both sad and sweet at the same time." Her gaze rested on the calico. "I can't blame you for not being able to choose. Truthfully? I don't know how Tony's going to pick just one dog after the festival." She took a couple steps until she was standing right in front of him. "You're doing a lot of good here, Brent. Don't ever second guess yourself."

Nicole's words warmed his heart. Probably way more than they should have. Being around her made him feel like he could be himself, something he appreciated.

He realized they were still standing there, studying each other. The cool thing about it? It felt natural and not the least bit awkward. There was a quality about Nicole that drew him in, made him want to spend more time getting to know her.

They both flinched when the bell rang, announcing a visitor. Brent tossed Nicole an apologetic look and then hurried to the front room to find an older man waiting for him.

"Hello. I'm Brent. Welcome to Finding Forever. Is there anything I can help you with?"

"My wife's been wanting a dog since ours passed away over the summer. She's reluctant to come herself, afraid it'll make her too sad. I thought I'd come choose one and surprise her."

"Oh, I'm sorry to hear of your loss. It's always hard to lose a pet like that. They become a member of the family."

The older gentleman nodded. "They sure do. I was hoping you might have a smaller dog. One that isn't too energetic."

Two different dogs came to mind and Brent smiled. "I may have a couple of possibilities. If you'll come this way, I'll introduce you."

A half hour later, the little Cavalier King Charles spaniel mix was going home with her new owner. Brent made notes in the little dog's file and slid it into the cabinet drawer marked "adopted" with a satisfied clink.

By the time Nicole and Tony's three hours were up, all the animals inside had sparkling cages. The dogs had gotten nice, long walks, and the cats and exotics had treats. Since Nicole and Tony had gotten everything figured out, Brent had a renewed excitement for the future of the shelter. Having that kind of help three days a week might even free him up to do some of the repairs the kennels outside desperately needed. He started a mental list.

"You two did a fantastic job. Seriously, thank you."

Nicole reached for the bottle of hand sanitizer on the counter and pumped some into her hand. Tony followed suit. "We're glad to help. It was fun."

Tony nodded emphatically. "I can't wait to come back tomorrow."

"I'm looking forward to seeing you guys tomorrow, too. Have a great afternoon." Brent pointed a finger at Tony. "Study hard."

Tony made a face. "I will."

Nicole chuckled. "Come on, kiddo. Let's go." She flashed one last smile in Brent's direction before leading her son out the front door.

Brent didn't realize he'd been staring after them until their vehicle drove out of view. He'd worked with a lot of volunteers at the shelter over the years. Yet, these last few hours had been some of the most enjoyable in a while. No doubt a big part of that was because of the company.

Since everything seemed under control, he thought he'd check his e-mail. The first thing that caught his eye was an e-mail from his cousin, Claire. She worked at Doggie Town, a daycare and rescue facility in Crescentville, New York. They'd been close as kids thanks to their mutual love for animals. She was also one of the few people he'd talked to about the financial status of Finding Forever.

Brent was thrilled when Claire suggested she could come down for the festival to volunteer at the adoption tent. She planned to take some of the animals back with her if they didn't find their forever families. This e-mail contained her travel plans, and now it was official. She'd be driving a long way, but Claire always was one for road trips and adventures. Not only would it be great to see his cousin, but the extra help was a huge relief.

Now, if only he could find more volunteers and adopt out a record number of pets during the festival, he'd be set. It was overwhelming. But between having help from Nicole and Tony plus now Claire's travel confirmation, things were improving.

His thoughts shifted to Nicole again. Having her around could easily become one of his favorite things about the week. Brent remembered her kindness toward the cats and pictured that beautiful smile of hers. Yeah, he could get used to working together.

~

Nicole pressed a finger to her temple and rubbed hard. It was Thursday night and the headache pulsing in her skull only pounded harder at her lame attempts to keep it at bay. She'd consulted a doctor and discovered it was probably stress-related. There was only so much she could do about it. She'd eased as much stress as possible. The rest? Well, that was just life.

The crack of wood on wood followed by a series of whoops pulled Nicole from the front counter to the rink. Tony was holding his hockey stick horizontally above his head, a grin on his face. Beads of sweat made their way down his cheeks to drip on his t-shirt. He glanced her way, and she gave him a thumbs up.

When he'd first played for the Wildcats in the local hockey league years ago, he'd been an intimidated and quiet kid. The sport had done a world of good in bringing him out of his shell. He'd since convinced two of his friends from their local homeschool group to play as well. The buddies always had fun during these practices and then the games every other Saturday.

Coach Jim gave the boys high fives and then suggested they get ready to face off again. Nicole checked the clock on her phone. Twenty more minutes until practice was over. Every tick of the clock seemed to make her headache worse. She was more than ready to get the place cleaned up and head for home. She looked forward to a hot shower with some of her favorite essential oils. Then she could relax and read one of the new books she'd bought. A perfect way to end the day.

Their second day volunteering at Finding Forever was as busy as the first. But Nicole thought she'd be right at home by the end of next week. She found she enjoyed caring for the animals, especially the cats. They'd only been volunteering for two days, and she was entertaining the possibility of adopting a cat as well as a dog for Tony. Boy, she must be tired.

Still, there was that long-haired calico who kept staring at Nicole with sad yellow eyes. Nicole couldn't resist, and stopped to talk to the cat frequently.

Brent was easy to work with. He had a lot of funny tales about animals at the shelter and several times today, she'd laughed until her eyes watered. She remembered Brent telling Jim stories when he used to come by for games, and how she'd appreciated his sense of humor even then.

Nicole hadn't realized how much she'd missed it until now. That thought sobered her right up. There were a lot of things about her future that changed when Stephen walked out, and she'd had no choice but to pack away many of her goals. Working here at the rink wasn't exactly a dream come true. But it was a job, and it was enough to provide a stable life for Tony.

No amount of wishing for more was going to change their circumstances. She would do what was best for her son, even if it meant she'd be working at the skating rink for the foreseeable future.

At least volunteering at the shelter was giving her a breath of fresh air she desperately needed. Just thinking about Brent caused her pulse to race, and she rolled her eyes at herself.

Tony finished his practice, and the kids headed for the benches. Jim approached her with a wave. "The kids are doing great. I wish they all could practice every day like Tony does." He gave one of the boys a hearty pat on the shoulder as he walked by. "Brent mentioned he stopped by earlier this week."

"He brought some flyers for me to put up. Tony and I are volunteering over at the shelter for a few weeks."

Jim's face lit up. "That's wonderful. It's good for kids to do something to help others." Cooper Rockford, one boy on the team, called the coach over. Jim gave him a nod. "See if you can convince Brent to stop by for a game or two."

"I'll see what I can do." The thought of Brent coming around more often caused her heart rate to increase in tempo. Annoyed with herself, she started cleaning up the rink area.

By the time Nicole got everything closed up, the headache was bad enough that nausea was rolling through her.

Tony put a hand on her shoulder. "You okay, Mom?"

She gave him what she hoped was a confident smile. "I'll be fine, buddy. It's just a headache. We'll get home, eat, and I'm sure it'll ease up."

He nodded but didn't seem convinced.

Once home, Nicole took an ibuprofen before warming up some leftover pizza.

The medication, a large glass of water, and food eased her headache some. Tony had curled up in the recliner with his gaming system, and Nicole was about ready to hop into the shower when her phone rang.

A quick glance at the caller ID and any sense of calm she'd built up since they got home evaporated. It was Mom. As tempted as Nicole was to ignore the call and let it go to voicemail, Mom would only call again. "It's Grandma," she called out to Tony before collapsing on her bed. With one arm over her eyes to block out the light above her, she answered the call. "Hey, Mom."

"Hi, Nicki. How are you and my favorite grandson doing tonight?"

"We're good. Tony had a blast at hockey practice." Nicole told her about volunteering at the local animal shelter, making a point of not mentioning Brent's name. For the last two years, Mom had been intent on getting Nicole to date again, insisting she wasn't getting any younger and that she needed help to raise Tony. Nicole strongly disliked all of it and would just as soon not add fuel to the fire.

"I think it'd be good for Tony to get a dog. It'll teach him some responsibility and be great company at home."

Nicole nodded her agreement. Thankfully, Mom shifted right into news about both of Nicole's siblings and what they were doing with their lives. Neither of them was married, but Mom was certain that Nicole's little sister's boyfriend would propose any day now.

"Have you met anyone new?"

And there it is. Nicole's mind wandered, and she took a moment to respond to her mom's question. "Um, no. Not really." Not a lie. She'd known Brent for a long time. But why his name had even come to mind bothered her as much as Mom's question.

"Have you thought about taking a class, honey? That's a good way to meet people."

Nicole sighed. "You know what, Mom? I should go. It's been a crazy day, and I have a killer headache. Can I call you this weekend?"

"Of course. You take care of that headache, and I'll talk to you later."

They said their goodbyes, and Nicole released a sigh. So much for burying her thoughts of Brent.

Well, she was counting down the days until they'd be back at the shelter next Tuesday. She wanted to see whether the calico had been adopted or not. It had absolutely nothing to do with the handsome man who ran the place. Now, if only she could truly convince herself of that.

~

The next Tuesday, Tony got through his morning schoolwork in record time in anticipation of getting back to the shelter. If he did his work like that regularly, Nicole just might sign them up to volunteer every day during the week. She laughed at the thought as her son threw open the passenger door and jumped into their car.

She got in and started it. Tony eyed the clock.

"We'll get there in plenty of time, kiddo. Your work ethic is impressive, though."

"I can't wait to walk the dogs again and play with them. How am I supposed to pick just one when the festival comes around?"

From the expression on Tony's face, it was clear he was worried about it.

"I don't know. But you'll figure it out. By then, one of the dogs will probably stand out from the others, and you won't doubt which one you should take home." Nicole hoped Tony might get a chance to interact with some of the larger dogs. She'd never been a huge fan of the toy breeds.

She knew how he felt, though. It would be difficult for her to choose only one animal to take home right now.

When they walked into the farmhouse, Brent waved at them from the counter with a phone to one ear.

"Yep. I've got some preparations to make today. You sure tomorrow will be okay? All right. We'll be ready."

He hung up the phone but continued writing something down on a piece of paper. A minute or two later, he glanced up, giving her a warm smile. "Sorry about that. I'm glad you're both here." He put the pen he was using in a mug and walked around the counter.

"What's going on?" Nicole could tell it was something major by the way Brent was rubbing the back of his neck. It looked like he had a million things going on in his head.

"There's a small farm on the other side of town that's been run by the same family for generations. Apparently, there's been a death in the family. Carl, the man who owns it, has to move across country and will be detained there indefinitely. He has animals that need to be re-homed. But because of the nature of the emergency, he doesn't have the means to do that before he leaves. He wants to bring the animals here because he knows we'll ensure they're taken care of."

Tony's eyes grew wide. "Farm animals?"

Brent nodded. "Two horses, a donkey, chickens, a pig. I'm not sure what else. But knowing Carl, they'll all be more like pets than livestock."

"Wow." Nicole tried to imagine where Brent would put the animals. They'd gotten a quick tour of the livestock already staying at Finding Forever last week. Would there be enough room for the new animals?

"I know. Anyway, let's focus on getting the cats, exotics, and indoor dogs taken care of. Then we can drive back to the barn and see what we can do to get ready."

Tony nodded in excitement. "I'll go get started!"

"Me, too." Nicole pulled a hairband out of her pocket and gathered her hair into a low ponytail.

"I appreciate it. I'll work through some plans in my head and make a couple of phone calls. Normally, I'd have the animals transferred to Blayne's place. But if he can't find them homes, he'll have to transport them back here for the festival, anyway. I'd rather save him a trip. Besides, I've known this guy releasing these animals for years, and I hate to do that since he's relying on this shelter to re-home them."

"Maybe most of them will find new families at the festival, if they don't find them beforehand." Nicole figured there had to be some farms around that would be happy to take in the chickens or horses. Perhaps even the donkey.

"I hope so. It's about to get interesting around here." He flashed a smile and squeezed her shoulder lightly as she walked by.

Her skin tingled at his touch. Getting interesting? That was an understatement.

Chapter Four

Brent leaned over the door and peered into the stall. Nicole stepped onto a hay bale to see what had his attention. Her arm brushed against his. "They told you one pig, huh?"

They watched as the mama pig shifted on the hay, four piglets vying for space at her teats as they made little oinks and snorts.

He laughed and shook his head. "Yeah. And I'm pretty sure these are pot-bellied." He checked the paperwork he had in his hands. "According to Carl, the mama's name is Winnie." She gave him a sorrowful look. Brent knew next to nothing about pot-bellied pigs, much less how to care for five of them. This wasn't at all what he was expecting. "I'll have to do some research. I have no idea when the piglets will be old enough to wean."

Nicole giggled. "Between these and having only one horse instead of two, I guess you're lucky there weren't more surprises."

"Isn't that the truth?" They migrated down to the stalls at the far end of the barn. The brown donkey moved closer to them, and Brent reached in to scratch his fuzzy ears. Carl had named the animal Kong, something they'd all gotten a good chuckle out of.

Kong obviously enjoyed the attention while the horse in the next stall eyed them nervously and backed away.

Nicole frowned. "What's wrong, big guy?"

The buckskin gelding just shook his head and snorted.

"Careful." Brent read the information he had about the horse again. "His name is Chance. Carl rescued the poor guy from an abusive situation, and it sounds like it took a while for Chance to settle down." Sadly, another change of hands might prove too much for the skittish horse. When Brent stepped closer to Nicole, Chance jerked and tried to back even further into the stall.

Brent held up two hands and moved away. He noticed that the more distance he put between himself and Chance, the less agitated the horse appeared. While Chance didn't seem to want Nicole to pet him, he also didn't appear to mind her as much. Maybe the gelding had issues with men? He'd make a note to caution Walt about the possibility.

"Hey, Mom!" Tony's voice called to them from one of the other stalls in the barn. "These Pygmy goats are awesome. I wish we had a farm. I'd totally want to take one of them home."

Brent followed Nicole, and they all laughed at the antics of the goat duo. Brent had to admit they were funny to watch. Prancing around and craving attention, they reminded him of dogs.

Ten chickens had come in with the other animals as well. But there was no way that he'd risk putting them with the other flock they were caring for already. If he did, odds were there'd be casualties. Brent did his best to create a makeshift coop outdoors. He hoped it'd hold them for a while.

Nicole turned her head and looked at Brent. A strand of hair blocked her view, and she tucked it behind an ear. "What's the plan?"

"Get through the next couple of days until Rob drops by on Friday. I'll have him examine all the animals and make sure everyone's healthy. Though it seems they were well taken care of."

Nicole nodded. "They do look good. And if they're given a clean bill of health?"

"I'll probably put pictures up on the website this week. It'd be best if I can find them homes before the festival." He tapped the side of the stall. "These guys look set for now. We need to get back to the farmhouse."

Tony hopped down. "Can I go visit the big dogs for a few minutes?"

Brent waited for Nicole's nod of approval before replying. "Go ahead. But don't let any of the dogs out of their kennels. If you'd like to help with them, Walt should be back from lunch shortly and maybe you can help him. Let Walt manage the two largest dogs."

"Yes, sir. Thanks, Mom!" Tony raced out of the barn with a grin on his face.

Brent had to wrangle the barn door closed. He walked side-by-side with Nicole back to the house.

Nicole cleared her throat. "Last week, you mentioned there were repairs that needed to be done. I can tell the barn is included in the list. What else?"

Brent took in a deep breath. More needed repairs than he wanted to admit. But money was limited, and there were only so many minutes in the day. It was one of the things that frustrated him most. "The house needs new paint. We need a new roof on the dog kennels outside, and we desperately need a second set of kennels to get those smaller dogs out, too. If they had indoor/outdoor kennels, it would reduce time spent walking them every day." He stopped walking and took in the surrounding land. "Mr. Rice wanted me to use this place for animal rescue, and I'm doing that. But by not keeping the place up to snuff, I feel like I'm failing him."

"I doubt that's true. One person can only do so much."

"Yeah, I know. But still, he never would've allowed it to get this bad."

Nicole nudged him in the arm with her elbow. "You've transformed this place from an old farmhouse to a sanctuary for animals that have nowhere else to go. I'm certain Mr. Rice would be proud of that."

She was watching him now, her blue eyes almost the same shade as the bits of sky peeking through the clouds. A breeze blew some of her red hair into her face. On instinct, he reached out and swept it away from her cheek.

The pulse in her neck quickened and seemed to match the way his heart was pounding inside his chest.

Nicole worried her bottom lip between her teeth and his attention went right to it. It was completely irrational, but Brent wanted to kiss her. He took a step and leaned toward her, her gaze drawing him in.

The distant sound of laughter floated to them from the kennels. Nicole inhaled sharply, her gaze fell, and Brent's heart dropped along with it. What had he been thinking?

~

Nicole took a deep breath and a big step back, realizing only then just how close they'd been. Wordlessly, they continued their walk.

Goosebumps peppered Nicole's arms, and she resisted the urge to cross them. Instead, she focused on the house drawing closer as they made their way across the field behind it. She heard the dogs barking from the kennel area. The sound of Tony laughing had pulled her back to reality moments before.

But even more, she was hyper aware of Brent walking beside her. He'd been about to kiss her, she was sure of it. And the worst part? She'd wanted him to.

Why did that scare her more than anything else? Talking to her mom the other day certainly hadn't helped. There'd only been a handful of guys interested in her over the last ten years. Every time she opened herself up to the possibility, their interest disappeared the moment they found out she had a son. Which was fine with her, because if they didn't want to be a part of Tony's life, she didn't want them to be in hers, either.

Not that she wanted to get back into the dating scene. She'd been content for years with the knowledge it would be just her and Tony. It was better that way, and no one got hurt.

So, what was going on with Brent? He obviously knew about Tony. Was Brent really interested? Or had that almost kiss taken him by surprise as much as it had her?

Maybe she'd read way too much into the moment. What if it'd been all her? Her face heated and now she doubted herself. It was best to move forward as if nothing happened. Because nothing had — it was all in her head.

Nicole bit back a groan of frustration and a twinge of disappointment. As they re-entered the farmhouse, she glanced at the clock. Forty-five minutes until she and Tony would return home. "I'll go check on the critters quickly."

Brent gave her a small nod, and she hurried down the hallway.

The moment she entered the cat room, the calico stood from her spot at the back of her kennel and came forward, meowing. Nicole sank to the floor and opened the door, more than happy to welcome the warm ball of fur onto her lap. The cat had no name on the crate, but Nicole had started calling her Callie.

"Hey, girl," Nicole whispered as she ran a hand over the cat's silky fur. "I hope you don't mind if I hide out for a few minutes." She took in Callie's contentment and wished she could set her own worries aside so easily.

It'd be simpler if what happened — or nearly happened — with Brent was all in her head. Otherwise, it could be a long two weeks if things got awkward between them. For the first time, Nicole doubted her decision to volunteer nine hours a week.

The kitty nuzzled Nicole's chin and purred. It was exactly what she needed. What they both needed.

~

"I wish we could do more to help the shelter." Tony appeared thoughtful as they ate a late dinner.

Nicole understood completely. They'd both left the shelter exhausted after all the excitement of the incoming livestock. Throw in the emotional turmoil from the almost, but probably non-existent, kiss, and Nicole was blinking to keep her eyes open. "There's a lot Mr. Todd needs to do around that place."

Tony nodded. "And not enough time, that's for sure." He scooped up a big forkful of spaghetti and slurped it. "Too bad we can't go for the whole weekend and help out."

Nicole should've reprimanded him about the slurping, but she let it slide. Besides, her mind was churning over what Tony had said. She wasn't sure how much help she and Tony would be. But what if they brought in extra hands? Within moments, different possibilities built upon themselves.

By the next morning, she had a plan of attack in place. Jim was always talking about building team spirit and working together. When she pitched her idea to him, he thought it was great. In fact, there wasn't a hockey game this Saturday. It would be the perfect day for the team to help the shelter. Jim agreed to call parents and arrange everything as soon as she checked with Brent. Everything was coming together faster than she'd thought possible.

Brent. Sentiments swirled around each other as if caught in a blender. She couldn't wait to tell him about Saturday and see what he thought. Yet, what if she went in there and things were horribly awkward after yesterday? In that case, spending a large part of Saturday together probably wasn't the best idea.

Nicole tried to squelch her apprehension and straightened her spine. This was for Finding Forever and all the animals in need of homes. She could deal with her emotional mess for two more weeks.

When they arrived at the shelter, Tony ran off to take care of the dogs like he'd been doing every day. He'd gotten to where, once he finished playing with the smaller dogs, he'd help Walt with the larger breeds after lunch.

Before Nicole left to check on the cats, she cleared her throat. "Brent, I had something I wanted to run past you."

"Oh?" Brent's brows rose in curiosity. He leaned against the counter and gave her his full attention.

Two more weeks. Just two more weeks. "As you know, Jim's always wanting to build up team spirit with the Wildcats." She slipped her hands into her pockets to keep from fidgeting. "I spoke with him, and he thought a team-building activity was just what the boys needed." She paused when Brent's eyes revealed his confusion. She hurried on to explain. "If it works out okay for you, a bunch of the boys would like to come on Saturday and help you with any repairs you might need. We've spoken with Sam over at Romance Hardware, and he's donating the supplies you need to repaint the main house."

Brent's mouth opened and then closed again. "Are you serious?"

Nicole grinned. "Absolutely. We want to spend Saturday painting the house, repairing anything that needs it, mowing, trimming bushes. Put a list of things together and be prepared to delegate."

Brent seemed lost. And for a moment, Nicole wondered if she'd completely overstepped her bounds.

She pulled her hands back out of her pockets and held one up. "If you'd rather we didn't come in and mess things up…"

"Oh, no. This is incredible. Seriously. Thank you, Nicole."

"You're welcome." Nicole couldn't take her gaze from his face. He looked relaxed, as if a giant weight had been lifted from his shoulders. "You never know, maybe some of the kids will want to come back and volunteer on a regular basis."

"That would be awesome." Brent rubbed his cheek with his hand, hiding his dimple, and shook his head. "You're amazing."

Nicole ducked her chin. "It wasn't just me. You're doing a lot of good here, and both Tony and I want to see it continue." She pulled her phone out of her pocket. "I'll text Jim and let him know we're good to go for Saturday."

Maybe the next two weeks wouldn't be as uncomfortable as she'd feared they'd be. Hope bubbled up inside and Nicole smiled. See? She and Brent could work together for the sake of the rescue center.

~

Brent watched as Nicole sent a text to Jim. He couldn't believe she'd done this for the shelter. For him. If they got the repairs made and spruced the place up a little… Well, it would put the center that much closer to having a stable future again. Maybe, if they got enough funds from the festival, he could even get that second set of kennels built sometime this coming spring. They'd have this place in shape again soon.

Brent pictured Mr. Rice nodding his head in satisfaction and smiled to himself.

He rummaged in a drawer for a piece of paper and jotted down the various jobs he had in mind for the boys on Saturday. He should probably feed them, especially if they worked all day long.

As if Nicole were reading his mind, she slipped her phone back into a pocket. "Della's Diner is donating lunch. Someone will deliver sub sandwiches along with chips and drinks."

Wow. She'd considered everything.

She gave him another smile and pointed toward the hall. "I'll go get started."

He watched her disappear. He'd been afraid things would be awkward after yesterday. But she'd come in with a way to help save Finding Forever. Not to mention that smile he couldn't get out of his head no matter what he did. It seemed everything was okay. Was it possible she felt the same pull between them that he did?

He spent a while composing his list of things he hoped to get accomplished on Saturday and then went to find Nicole. She was sitting on the floor of the cat room, the calico curled up in her lap. She kept running a hand over the cat's fur, a far-off look in her eyes.

"You're deep in thought."

His voice startled her and the cat. Both turned their heads to study him. Nicole shrugged. "Sorry, I know I'm taking too long in here today." She stood and eased the calico back into her temporary home. "I got distracted."

"Are you kidding?" Brent took several steps nearer. "You arranged a miracle for this place. You deserve a few minutes to take a breather." He looked around the room. "Mr. Rice would get a kick out of the kids coming to help on Saturday. If he were still here, I have no doubt he'd welcome them with jugs of lemonade and lollipop trees."

Nicole looked amused. "Lollipop trees?"

Brent nodded and moved to lean against the wall. "He used to create them every Halloween. He'd buy lollipops that came in strips of plastic. The handles would stick either to the left or the right. If you wanted a lollipop, you just walked up and pulled it out of the plastic packaging." He grinned. "Mr. Rice would hang those all over the trees out front, and he'd tell the little kids the lollipops actually grew on trees. Everyone who trick-or-treated at his house was welcome to take one."

"That sounds really neat. Every neighborhood needs a guy like Mr. Rice."

"I couldn't agree more."

Mr. Rice would've liked Nicole. In fact, Brent could easily imagine Mr. Rice teasing him, insisting Nicole was a looker and Brent should snag her before some other guy did.

Yep, Mr. Rice would've been right, too. Brent would be an idiot to not want to spend more time with her.

Chapter Five

Nicole still smiled in response to the memory Brent shared about the lollipop trees. It sounded like Mr. Rice was truly the neighborhood grandfather. She almost wished she'd grown up on this street, too, just to have the opportunity to meet him.

She realized Brent was watching her, his expression open. What was he thinking about? She tried to interpret the softness in his eyes.

Brent opened his mouth as though he were going to say something when Tony ran in. "Mr. Todd, Walt sent me to tell you we need some help. Costello got his leg caught up in the fence."

"Why am I not surprised?" Brent raised an eyebrow at Nicole as if to say the conversation wasn't over.

Her cheeks flushed, and she tilted her head toward Tony. "I'll lock the front door. Go ahead."

"Thanks."

Brent followed Tony out at a jog. Nicole got everything secured, put a sign on the door, and then made her way to the kennels behind the house. There was no missing the giant dog lying on his side in the grass. Tony, Walt, and Brent had kneeled beside him. Nicole hastened her steps. "Is he going to be okay?"

Costello raised his large head and watched her out of the corner of his eye. He let his head drop again with a long, dramatic groan.

Brent ran his hands down Costello's front, right leg until the dog whined. "I think he probably broke it. Rob comes in first thing tomorrow morning. It'd be better to keep him in a kennel with limited movement until then instead of trying to get him to the office today."

Walt nodded. "I wouldn't want to get him to stay still in a car for anything."

Tony moved to the dog's head and kept rubbing his ears. "What were you thinking, boy?"

"How'd this happen?" Nicole saw nothing obvious he might have injured himself on.

Walt chuckled. "He didn't want to wait for me to open his kennel and tried to climb over the partially opened gate. He got his paw stuck in that bent section."

Nicole had no problem imagining Costello climbing the gate. He'd probably scale a six-foot fence without thinking twice. Assuming he didn't simply clear it with a leap. The dog was a beast.

"I hope we can get this guy adopted at the festival." Brent stood. "When he pulls stunts like this..." He shook his head. "Combine his large size with his energy level, and now a messed-up leg, we'll be lucky if anyone gives him a second look."

Tony was still rubbing the dog's ears, and Costello moved his head to rest it on the boy's lap. Nicole bit back a sigh. She had put no limitations on the dog Tony could adopt once the festival began. But now she wished she had. He was getting attached to Costello. What on earth would they do with a dog that was bigger than she was? Not to mention he was apparently an escape artist to boot. This wasn't the time to bring it up. Not with Brent and Walt around. And not when her son was so determined to keep the dog calm.

Brent motioned toward the house. "Walt, will you go get an extra blanket for Costello's kennel? Let's hope he can refrain from chewing it to bits until tomorrow."

"You got it, boss." Walt dusted off his pants and headed for the house at a jog.

"I'll try to fix the spot he got his paw caught in. It was on the list to repair Saturday." Brent stared down at Costello. "You couldn't wait two more days before getting into trouble, huh, big guy?"

"We've got him," Nicole assured Brent and sat down on the grass beside Tony. Costello groaned and rolled his eyes. She laughed. "You really are a big baby, aren't you?"

"Mom, it's sad that he's been here this long because no one wants him." He lifted his brown eyes to hers. "Maybe we could take him with us."

Nicole was hoping to put this conversation off until they got back home. But with her son watching her like that, she had little choice. "Honey, I don't think we'd have a big enough yard to keep him happy. The fence is certainly not tall enough to contain him. And he'd go through our house like a tornado."

"Yeah, I know." Tony kept rubbing Costello's ears. The dog's eyes drifted closed, and he released a deep sigh.

"It's hard seeing so many animals that need homes, isn't it?" Nicole leaned over far enough to let her shoulder bump into Tony's. "We can't adopt them all. But you are making a difference by spending time with the dogs and helping Brent like you are."

Tony shrugged. "I guess."

Nicole was sure he understood. But when you're a kid, it didn't seem like enough. Truthfully, it didn't seem like enough to Nicole, either.

Walt returned and helped Brent set up the kennel area. When they were ready, Tony coaxed Costello to stand and led him inside. Costello limped, holding his leg high.

"Mom, can I eat lunch in here and keep an eye on him?"

Walt tilted his head toward a nearby kennel. "I'll be around. I still have several of these guys to take care of."

Nicole nodded. "That's fine. But make sure *you* eat your sandwich." She raised a knowing eyebrow at him. He agreed. "All right. Stay here and I'll bring your lunch back in a few minutes."

~

Brent picked Stormy up off the counter and set her down on the floor for the fourth time. He and Nicole were trying to eat a rushed lunch of sandwiches and chips, and the cat was insistent she should get a bite or two.

Stormy glared up at him with her yellow eyes before sauntering off, her tail twitching.

Brent pointed at her. "And that's why I set nothing on this counter. She's been known to pay me back for angering her."

Nicole covered her mouth, swallowed her bite of food, and gave a quiet laugh. "She does have quite the personality."

"I'd go with attitude." But Brent didn't mind. She was sweet most of the time and a great mouser. Most people got a kick out of her greeting them at the door.

He polished off the last of his chips. "So, are you and Tony are coming on Saturday?"

"Of course." Nicole smiled.

"Good. What all do you and Tony have planned for tomorrow?"

She crumpled up her napkin and stuffed it into an empty sandwich bag. "The rink holds a late night open skate every Friday evening. It's always packed. We'll be there until closing at ten." Her voice sounded tired as she relayed the information.

How did she keep up with everything? Between raising Tony, educating him, and keeping a full-time job that included a lot of late evenings and Saturdays, no wonder the poor girl was exhausted.

~

The next evening, Brent walked into the skating rink, the sounds of families having fun filling the room. He waited for his turn to approach the window where Nicole was one of two people accepting money for admission. When she noticed him, she froze in place as her eyes widened.

"What are you doing here?"

He gave her a winning smile. "I thought I'd check out this late-night skate."

"You're going to skate?"

Brent raised himself up, so he was standing as tall as possible. "I'll have you know I was quite the skater back in the day."

Nicole pressed her lips together but couldn't keep a smile at bay. "Regular or inline?"

"Inline, please." He placed the correct amount of money on the counter and pushed it toward her. She took it and placed a stamp on the back of his hand. "Go on in."

Brent remembered enough about roller skating in the past to wear tall, thick socks. Sometime later, he was also reminded how tired his ankles got when he hadn't skated in a long time. And while it was much like riding a bike, and he'd avoided making a fool of himself for the most part, it was still exhausting. Not to mention awkward, especially when it came to stopping with any measure of grace.

The waist-high wall that surrounded most of the rink absorbed his halt. Tony stopped expertly and grinned at him. "You're pretty good, Mr. Todd."

"Thanks, Tony. I can tell you practically live on skates."

Tony nodded. "I've had to get two new pairs this year because I keep wearing them out."

Brent pointed toward Nicole who was still busy with all the customers. "Does your mom ever get a break on Friday nights?"

"We stop taking new people at eight and then she usually has a lot more time." With that, Tony pushed off the floor and was back on the rink skating to eighties music.

Brent checked the time. With over a half hour until Nicole would get a breather, he decided he'd better sit down for a while. Otherwise, he'd be done before he even got a chance to spend time with her. He found a spot at one of the few picnic-style tables on one end and enjoyed watching all the people skate, laugh, and visit.

A while later, a shadow fell on him and stopped. Nicole stood in front of him, hands on her hips and inline skates on her feet. "I'm surprised you're still here."

Brent shrugged. "Sometimes I don't know when to quit." He gave her a pointed stare and was satisfied to see pink creep up her neck and into her face. "You've been working hard."

She glanced over at the front desk. "The hardest part of my evening is over. Natalie will keep an eye on the front counter for the rest of the evening. Now I just need to stay awake."

"If there are no more people coming in, what do you do for the rest of the evening?"

"I'm mostly a chaperone. Concessions and the skate counter are manned by other people." She pointed toward the DJ. "And I could only choose the music once before getting kicked out of that spot." They laughed. "I usually end up skating for a while and visiting with people. But yeah, Friday nights are long ones by the time we clean up and close."

"So, if I head back onto the rink, I might run into you out there?" He crossed his arms in front of him, well aware he'd presented a dare.

She shrugged but couldn't quite keep the amusement from her face. "Maybe."

The DJ put on the original Ghostbusters song and most of the people on the rink cheered and sang along. Brent laughed. "I haven't heard that one in ages."

"Trust me, if you stick around here in the evenings, you'll hear many songs from your childhood."

Brent stood and skated onto the rink, happy to see Nicole was right behind him. They joined the crowd and skated side-by-side for a while. Ten minutes later, the DJ announced it was now couples only, and you had to be holding hands to stay on the rink.

A lot of people found a partner to skate with whether it was a parent, sibling, friend, or spouse. Brent held a hand out to Nicole. "Don't leave me out here all by myself." He winked.

She shook her head at him as if she didn't quite know what to do with him before sliding her hand into his. The surrounding air had chilled her skin as they'd skated, and he liked the idea of warming it back up again. He laced their fingers together and gave her hand a squeeze. This felt right; as if her hand belonged in his.

They skated past the tables as Tony took a seat at one of them. "I take it your son isn't a fan of couple's skate."

Nicole laughed at that and seemed relieved to have something else to focus on. "Oh, no. He's at the age where the thought of participating in any way may as well signal the end of life as we know it."

Brent chuckled. "I remember those days."

"Yep, I'm fine with them. I'm not ready for him to grow up yet. Girlfriends, jobs, etc. I want to hold onto my boy a little longer if I can."

They made their way around the rink as Brent studied her profile. "I'm surprised there aren't guys lined up waiting to skate with you tonight."

Nicole noticeably picked up the pace and seemed to look anywhere else but him. He'd assumed she was still single. What if that wasn't the case? The thought of anyone else out here holding her hand caused a mix of protectiveness and jealousy to rise in his chest. When Nicole said nothing, he tugged on her hand just enough to slow her down. She glanced at him.

Brent had to know, even if roller skating might not be the most appropriate place to ask. "Are you seeing anyone?"

She gave her head a little shake. "No."

Who knew one little word could inspire such a sense of relief? He flashed her a smile. "Good."

The song signaling couples skate ended way too quickly as far as Brent was concerned, and the DJ welcomed everyone else back onto the floor. Brent didn't want to let go of Nicole's hand, but he released it. They skated a little while longer before deciding to sit down again.

Nicole leaned back with her elbows resting on the table top behind her. "It's always nice to see the families come in together on Friday nights. What about you? Any relatives in the area?"

Brent's feet ached, and he decided that was about all the skating he would be up to. He loosened the buckles on the inline skates and slid his feet out, breathing a sigh of relief. "Not here in Romance. My family is scattered all over the place, the closest being my mom, an aunt, and one of my brothers in Portland. How about you?" He knew a little about Nicole's past, but not nearly as much as he'd like to.

"No family here. I grew up in Idaho in a little town a lot like this where everyone knows everyone else. After everything with Tony's dad... Tony and I were on our way to Portland, stopped in Romance for a bite to eat, and fell in love with the town. It seemed like a good place to get a fresh start." Her eyes focused on something in the distance. "This is the only home Tony has ever known." She finally cleared her throat and sat up straight.

"Was your family understanding about you moving?"

"They understood but weren't happy with the decision. My mom tried to convince us to go back for years, but she gets it. We go stay for two weeks every summer. But our life is here in Romance. Tony's grown up here, and he has a lot of friends."

Her voice trailed off and Brent resisted the urge to put an arm around her shoulders. "You were brave. And you did what you needed to do to take care of your son. You should be proud of yourself." He nodded toward Tony as he passed by. "He's obviously happy, and he's a very helpful and respectful young man. You're doing a great job with him."

Nicole smiled brightly and twisted some hair around a single finger. "I appreciate that. I truly do." She brought her hands to her lap and clasped them together. "Do you see your mom much?"

Brent laughed. "Pretty regularly. She's always trying to play matchmaker." When Nicole nodded understandingly, he latched onto the small bit of information. "I take it your mom is the same way?"

"Oh, yes. I think that topic comes up more than our moving back to my hometown does." She shook her head. "Mom doesn't get that most guys I meet won't want a ready-made family. You know?"

"I'm sorry to hear guys never give you and Tony a chance. It's definitely their loss."

Nicole said nothing but shifted a little closer, their arms brushing against each other. It sent his heart racing, and he wondered if she was having the same reaction.

He'd always admired Nicole and thought she was beautiful. But now… Brent doubted he'd ever tire of her company. Could he convince her to give him even half a chance to prove he wasn't like the other guys she'd referred to?

Chapter Six

Saturday started off with a bang. Fifteen of the kids from the hockey club arrived along with five dads willing to help. Nicole and two other women kept busy caring for the smaller animals and coordinating groups. Meanwhile, the guys jumped right into the work and repairs needed for Finding Forever.

By the time lunch arrived, the lawn had been cut and edged, bushes trimmed, and the house siding prepared for a new coat of paint.

It reminded Nicole of the way communities used to come together to raise a barn or repair a house damaged by storms. It was amazing what could be accomplished when people worked together like this.

Everyone took a break and were busy devouring the sub sandwiches. Brent accepted a plastic cup of lemonade from Nicole, his fingers brushing hers in the process. "Aren't you going to sit down and eat?"

Since it seemed everything had been taken care of, Nicole shrugged. "Yeah, I guess I might as well." She grabbed her own lemonade, chose a turkey sandwich, and joined Brent at one of the long tables on the lawn behind the shelter.

The sun shone with no rain predicted for that day or the next. A perfect time to paint the house. Not only that, but everyone would accomplish a lot more if they weren't worried about getting wet.

She nodded toward the house. "So, I saw someone marking up the side of the house. What's up with that?"

Brent swallowed and chuckled. "We may not be able to get another outdoor kennel set up anytime soon. But Leo's going to install a door at the end of the hall so we can walk the dogs right outside. He should have it all cut out and installed before we're ready to paint that side of the house."

Nicole thought about how they walked the dogs through the house and out the back now. "Wow, that'll save a lot of time."

"Yep!" Brent took a large bite of his roast beef sandwich.

Nicole was starving, and she hadn't been working nearly as hard as all the guys had been. It was a good thing Della's Diner sent enough sandwiches. "Is there anything I can do to help once we get all of this cleaned up?"

"You are helping a great deal keeping track of the animals inside. If you can check on Costello, that would be great. Make sure he hasn't figured out how to get out of that cone."

Nicole laughed. After the vet had put the dog's foot in a cast, poor Costello had been given the cone of shame to keep him from chewing the cast off. Costello was proof that it was quite possible for a dog to mope. "I'll be happy to check on him."

"Thanks." Brent grinned at her. A bunch of the guys finished their lunch and deposited paper plates in the trash. Brent polished off his own, dusted his hands off, and squeezed her shoulder as he stood. "Back to work we go. I'll come find you in a while."

Nicole waved. It was fun to see him this happy. And after years of trying to keep the shelter going, he deserved help like this. The others were enjoying it as well. She caught Tony's eyes and lifted a thumbs up. He returned it enthusiastically before jogging toward the back of the house with teammate Cooper where two of the adults were opening cans of paint.

Brent appeared, a folded step ladder under one arm. He carried it as if it didn't weigh a thing. She realized she was staring when someone cleared their throat and repeated themselves. Cheeks warm, Nicole jumped to her feet and forced herself to focus on clearing the tables.

It was over an hour before she excused herself to go check on Costello. Thankfully, she found him behaving himself and moping pathetically. Those big eyes rolled upward as he gave her his best sad dog impersonation. "I know, guy. But if you hadn't been in such a hurry, you wouldn't have hurt yourself in the first place." Despite all attempts to guard against it, Costello was worming his way into her heart.

Nicole wandered through to make sure all the dogs still had water. After that, she went down to the barn to check on the animals there. The chickens happily pecked the ground in their makeshift coop outside. Sounds of the goats bleating welcomed her into the barn. Since they were so insistent, she checked on them first. She was tempted to open the door to the stall and pet them, but she was afraid one of them might escape.

Next, she ran a hand over Chance's soft nose and then rubbed Kong's ears. Both would be allowed to roam in the fenced pasture behind the barn once everyone else left. They'd discovered Kong lived up to the stereotype and didn't seem to care much for dogs. Brent thought it best to keep both larger animals in the stalls until that evening.

Her last stop was the pot-bellied pigs. She had to admit, they'd quickly worked their way to the top of her favorite animals list. Though she couldn't fathom owning one. Sure, the four little guys were adorable, but if they got as big as their mama…

Nicole stood on tiptoes to see over the edge of the railing. The mama pig grunted her welcome. The babies were busy drinking milk or rooting around in the hay.

Wait, only three? Where was the fourth piglet?

Nicole looked around and spotted a stool. She brought it over to the stall and stood on it for a better viewpoint. Her heart plummeted when once again, she only counted three of them. "Now where did you go?" She was about to panic when she leaned over and saw the little guy snuffling around the bottom of the stall door as if looking for a way out. "Don't even think about it." The piglet, white with brown spots, lifted his pink nose as if ready to defy her. "I thought you'd gotten out. You shouldn't scare people like that, you know."

She shifted her weight and without warning, the stool toppled. Just as Nicole expected to fall, strong arms came around her and caught her on the way down. Before she knew it, she was being placed on her feet again. She turned to find Brent grinning at her, his arms still wrapped around her waist.

~

Brent resisted a chuckle as Nicole's eyes grew wide. "You should take your own advice about not scaring people. It's a good thing I was here."

Nicole's head turned, and she took in the stool lying on its side on the ground. "I'm glad you were, too."

He liked that her cheeks turned pink, and she hadn't moved to step out of his arms. "What were you doing?"

"I thought one of the piglets was missing. I was trying to spot it before going in. The little guy was only hiding." Her gaze turned back to him. "Mental note not to stand on that stool again. What are you doing here?"

Holding her in his arms was amazing. That was probably a bad thing, right? If it were, he didn't care. "Searching for you. I didn't see you around the house, and Costello acted like he'd lost his best friend. I figured you might have come here. The door is about finished and everyone's taking a breather, so I wanted to make sure you didn't need any help."

Nicole nodded. "All's fine." Her blue eyes fixed on his. "I guess we'd better be getting back, then, before break time is over."

"Yeah, we probably should."

Except neither of them moved. Her gorgeous eyes pulled him in. Before Brent knew what he was doing, he'd leaned in closer. The scent of her shampoo combined with the hay in the barn, promising a memory he wasn't likely to forget. When she tilted her chin up, he pressed his lips to hers. The kiss melded together the gentleness he associated with Nicole and a fire he'd never experienced before. Nothing else existed as he explored her satiny lips.

One goat bleated, and they both jumped. Nicole let her forehead fall against his chest. He brushed a kiss on the top of her head and then took her hand in his. "I think that's our cue." He used his other hand to right the stool and then led the way out of the barn. "I wish we didn't have to go back for a while."

"Yeah." Nicole's voice sounded nervous, and as they neared the crowd, she opened her hand and let it fall away from his.

He frowned. Was she worried someone might see them? It wasn't like he'd planned it, but when the beautiful woman he couldn't stop thinking about literally fell into his arms...

The possibility that she might regret their kiss hit him like a cheap shot to the ribs. Kissing her was something he'd wanted to do for a while. He didn't regret it. In fact, he'd duplicate it right now if he had the chance.

He'd just decided to stop and ask if she was okay when Leo spotted them and waved Brent over. He swallowed his frustration and ignored the unease building in the pit of his stomach.

Brent glanced at Leo who was waiting for him and then back at Nicole. "Duty calls. See you in a while?"

She nodded, her expression conflicted.

It took nearly all of Brent's willpower to readjust his focus onto his friend. Leo was excited to show him what they'd done with the new entrance. Brent had no doubt Leo knew what he was doing. But examining the door now, it looked like it'd existed all along. A small set of wooden steps were placed below the landing, allowing much easier access outside.

"This looks great, Leo. How can I thank you?"

Leo tilted his head toward the house. "Did I hear right that you have chickens?"

Brent nodded. "I do. Two different flocks of them. I don't suppose you'd be interested in one or two."

"I'll take a whole flock. We've got a chicken coop and could use more."

"They're yours." The men shook hands. "I can't thank you enough. The time you're saving me daily is a big thing."

"We're glad to help."

The painting crew came around the corner, ready to tackle the final side of the house. Brent would paint the trim himself in a few days. It was amazing what this group had accomplished.

Several of the boys and the women were busy washing paintbrushes and working on something else Brent couldn't quite see. It only took him a moment to spot Nicole. She was laughing at something Tony said. Before long, the two were flinging water at each other from the newly-cleaned paintbrushes. Within moments, everyone there was having a water fight.

Brent laughed as he watched their antics. He thought back to what Nicole said about the previous men in her life.

Truthfully, any guy would be lucky to have both Nicole and Tony in his life. He only hoped he hadn't jeopardized any chance he had with her by kissing her when he did.

~

"Hey, stranger!"

Nicole's head lifted, and she smiled the moment she spotted her friend, Audrey. "Hey, yourself. What are you doing here? You know you've missed most of the party."

Audrey nodded. "Yeah, I'd heard through the grapevine a bunch of you were fixing up the place. I would've stopped by earlier, but I had an emergency call from one of my clients."

As one of the best psychologists in Romance, Audrey often stayed busy. They used to meet up for coffee occasionally, but it'd been a while. "Well, I'm glad you came by." Nicole pointed to the fading water drops on her shirt. "Too bad you didn't make it for the water fight."

Audrey's eyes widened. "In that case, I got here just in time." They laughed. "Is there anything I can help with?"

Nicole jabbed a thumb at the table that held the food. "You can help me wrap up whatever's left. I think everyone will be leaving shortly. We've gotten a lot done in a relatively short amount of time."

The friends walked over to the table. Except for a couple people walking by as they carried cans of paint to Leo's truck, they were alone.

Audrey wrapped up a sub sandwich. "What's new with you?"

Without even meaning to, Nicole's head came up and her gaze found Brent's. He waved at her and she waved back. She knew her cheeks had turned red, too, when Audrey's face broke into a grin. Nicole gave her a pointed stare. "Don't start, girl."

Audrey shook her head. "Are you kidding me? That's Brent, right? He's hot. Rob and Allie have talked about what a great guy he is. Good for you."

Nicole cast a furtive glance around her, making sure no one else was within earshot. "Shhhh, I don't want anyone else to hear. Especially Tony."

With a frown, Audrey paused what she was doing. "Don't they get along?"

"It's not that. Tony thinks Brent can do no wrong. But there's a difference between Brent being a mentor or…"

"His new daddy?" It was clear by Audrey's bright grin that she was teasing.

"You're not helping, you realize that, right?" Nicole shot her a look of desperation. "Seriously, Audrey. What if things don't work between us? Tony knows his father wanted nothing to do with him. If he gets attached to Brent and then something happens…" She groaned. Yep, she sounded pretty messed up.

"I get that. But is it fair to assume Brent is anything like Stephen? I'd hate for you to let fear sabotage something that could be amazing."

Nicole put plastic wrap over the remains of a vegetable plate. "Please don't psychoanalyze me, Audrey. I'm aware that I'm overreacting, but that's better than risking everything we have here." She swallowed down the lump in her throat. "I can't do that to Tony."

"Or yourself?" Audrey took several steps and gave her friend a hug.

There was no stopping a few tears from escaping. Nicole sniffed and swiped them away before anyone else saw, especially the two men in her life. "Thanks." She cleared her throat and tried to regain her composure before she and Audrey went back to wrapping stuff up. "So seriously, what do I do?"

"Talk to Tony. He's a smart kid. It doesn't have to be anything about getting married. Ask him what he thinks of Brent and go from there."

Nicole had different conversation scenarios swirling around in her head. What if Tony objected to the idea of Brent taking a bigger part in their lives? She wasn't sure she could do it.

"Nicole?"

"Hmmm?"

"It'll be okay."

~

"So, what do you think?" Brent looked to Tony on his left and Nicole on his right. Everyone else had gone home, and it was the three of them now, observing the finished house for the first time. The chipped and stained white paint had been removed and the siding covered with gray. When the maroon trim was added, it wouldn't even look like the same place. He thought Howard Rice would be happy with the result.

"The house is awesome!" Tony nodded his satisfaction. "My arm is killing me, though." He rubbed his right wrist for emphasis.

Brent smiled at him. "I sure appreciate all of your help. We couldn't have done this without you." He caught Nicole's gaze. "Either of you."

"Mom, can I go see Costello? Please?"

"Sorry, kiddo. We need to get home. It's getting late."

"But the festival is two weeks from today." Tony's happy face morphed into a sad frown. "I want to make sure his leg's doing okay."

Nicole walked around Brent to give her son a hug and ruffle his hair. "I know. But I checked on him earlier, and he's resting. You don't want to wake him up. He needs to sleep to get better. Besides, we have Skype with Grandma in an hour."

Tony brightened. "I almost forgot! Wait until I tell her what we did today." He turned to Brent. "Bye, Mr. Todd. We'll be back on Tuesday."

Brent shook the boy's hand. He wouldn't see either of them for two days. Right now, that seemed like forever. "Thanks again for your help, Tony. Have fun visiting with your Grandma."

"I will!" He grinned and jogged toward the car.

Brent turned to Nicole. "I hope you guys can take it easy tomorrow. You both deserve it."

She nodded. "I hope so, too. I guess you rarely get to relax much."

"Tomorrow won't be too bad. Besides, Leo's coming by to pick up one flock of chickens. That'll be good. Rob gave the all-clear on the rest of the farm animals, and I'll get their pictures up on the website tomorrow if I can." He paused. "I'll see you next week?"

"We'll be here."

She gave him a little smile, said goodbye, and hurried to the car where Tony was waiting.

Brent had to fight back the disappointment building in his chest. Nicole and Tony had only promised to volunteer until the festival was over. The clock was ticking, and his chance with Nicole was slipping through his fingers. Even worse, there wasn't a thing he could do about it.

Chapter Seven

Nicole got a kick out of listening to Tony tell Mom about the day at the shelter. He went on and on about Costello and helping Brent paint. In fact, by the time Tony was ready to go take his shower before bed, he'd referenced "Mr. Todd" a lot. When he'd left, Nicole moved into the middle of the screen. By Mom's telling expression, she'd caught it, too.

"So, who is this Mr. Todd?" She grinned mischievously.

"Mom, I've told you. That's Brent. He's the one who runs the Finding Forever Animal Rescue. Tony loves helping with all the animals."

"It sounds like he wishes he could take Costello home with him."

"Yeah, he does. But can you imagine a Great Dane in this house?" Nicole spread her arms wide to encompass their relatively small living room.

Mom busted out laughing. "Oh, I can imagine it. It's not a pretty sight. Does he know he can't pick Costello?"

"I've told him. But it's obvious that's the dog he really wants. I feel bad about it." Nicole frowned. "Plus, the poor thing has been in the shelter for six months as it is. I'm hoping he'll find a home at the festival, and everything will work itself out."

"Me, too. And what about Brent?"

"What about him?"

Mom shot her a look as though she were reminding Nicole that she wasn't born yesterday. "Tony seems pretty taken with him. Is he the only one?"

Nicole shifted in her seat, and there was no denying her interest. Especially when it came to Mom who could see right through any objections. She could only hope their Skype connection wasn't clear enough for Mom to detect the change.

No such luck. "I knew it! Oh, Nicki, that's great!"

Okay, she was blowing this way out of proportion. "Don't get too excited, Mom. We're just friends." Nicole wasn't sure what they were right now.

"I know I'm always bugging you about finding someone to share your life with. But in all seriousness, if you care about him, you've got to give it a chance to see if it works out. If you don't, you'll always wonder."

Now that was true. Nicole tried to steer the conversation toward one of her siblings and they soon said goodbye before logging off.

A ping from her phone announced an incoming text. Nicole expected it to be from her mom, remembering something she'd meant to tell her on Skype. Instead, it was Brent.

Thanks again for everything you two did. Tell Tony I checked on Costello, and he's sleeping like a baby. See you on Tuesday.

His message warmed Nicole's heart, and she couldn't hold back a smile.

I'll tell him. Thanks, Brent. Good night.

Good night.

~

Nicole swept the last of the glass into the dustpan and stood. The chime sounded, and Brent walked in through the front door of the shelter.

His brows creased. "What happened?"

Nicole held up the dust pan. "Stormy." She dumped the contents into the wastebasket. "She wouldn't quit bothering the rabbits. I made her leave the exotics room while I cleaned the cages. Apparently, I offended Her Majesty because she knocked my coffee mug off the counter."

Brent cringed. He investigated the room, but the cat was nowhere to be seen. "I'm sorry. I'll buy you another one."

"It's not a big deal. For whatever reason, my youngest sister insists on buying me a new coffee mug every year. I've got quite the collection." Nicole put the broom and dustpan away, overly aware of Brent's presence in the room.

It'd been that way since she and Tony had arrived two hours ago. Neither Brent nor Nicole had brought up the kiss on Saturday. But it was impossible to ignore the elephant in the room. She wasn't sure what she'd hoped for this morning. That he would kiss her the moment Tony left to care for the dogs? That Brent would give her the cold shoulder?

Brent was watching her closely, and Nicole covered her embarrassment by reaching for a piece of paper. "Someone called about the goats and said they'd be by later today." She handed the paper to Brent.

"Thank you." He grasped one side of the note. For a few moments, they both held it and neither moved. His gaze settled on her face. "Hey, Nicole. About the other day…"

The new side door opened and closed as Tony came inside. Brent pocketed the note, and Nicole took a small step back. Moments later, Tony jogged into the room. "That new exit makes all the difference in the world." He ran a hand through his hair. "I'm going to go see Costello. Is that cool?"

Nicole reached out and fixed some hair that was sticking up. He desperately needed a trip to the barber. "Of course."

"Thanks, Mom!" With a grin, he darted for the door and disappeared in moments.

"I remember having that much energy." Brent chuckled.

"Me, too. A long time ago." Nicole shook her head with a wistful smile.

He tilted his head in the direction Tony had gone. "I don't know. You seem to keep up with him just fine."

Nicole's heart did a little jig. "Thanks."

"He's a good kid." Brent tugged at one of his ears and then dropped his hand again. "I've been wanting to apologize for dropping off the radar this last year. It was never my intention. When I saw you guys at the rink a couple of weeks ago, I couldn't believe how much Tony had grown. That's when I realized how much can change in such a short amount of time." He hesitated. "I thought, once you guys finished volunteering, maybe I could stop by the rink regularly."

Brent focused on Nicole, his brown eyes filled with hope.

She swallowed and nodded. "I'd like that."

His mouth lifted in a grin. "Good." Brent moved closer. His hands settled on her shoulders, slipped down her arms, and finally cradled her elbows.

It wasn't the coolness of his skin that sent chills racing up her arm and down her spine. Nicole suppressed a shiver. His gaze focused on her lips, and she wet her own in anticipation.

The door chime sounded as a woman in her twenties walked in. Brent gave Nicole an apologetic look before turning to greet her. With a whoosh, Nicole blew out the breath she'd been holding and escaped to one of the cat rooms. She leaned against the wall and groaned.

She'd wanted Brent to kiss her even though Tony could've come into the room at any time. Not good. How was it possible for her head to blare warning after warning while her heart simultaneously sang with joy?

~

Brent never thought he'd complain about having too many volunteers. Word had gotten out about the work day at the shelter. By Thursday morning, a dozen people came in and scheduled time to volunteer.

It was more than he'd hoped for and was desperately needed. But it also meant he had no time alone with Nicole while she and Tony were at the shelter. Between that and her busy evenings working at the rink, Brent was craving time for them to talk.

Nicole and Tony were getting ready to leave for the day. Brent broke away from one of the newest volunteers to tell them goodbye.

Tony got hand sanitizer and rubbed it between his hands. "Hey, Mr. Todd. I have a hockey game on Saturday. Do you want to come? It's at ten in the morning."

Brent took in the boy's excitement and the guarded hope on Nicole's face. Right now, he'd give almost anything to say he'd be there. "I would in a flash, buddy. Except I have a meeting with the festival committee that morning."

Tony's face fell in disappointment. He rubbed the tip of his shoe against the bottom edge of the counter. His head snapped up, a grin replacing his frown. "What about my practice tonight?"

Nicole reached over and put a hand on his shoulder. "Mr. Todd has a lot going on right now, Tony."

Unsure whether it was the boy's enthusiasm or Nicole's acceptance of the situation that affected Brent more, he held up a hand. "I may be a little late. But I'll swing by and watch you play as soon as I close up here."

"Yes!" Tony's eyes sparkled. "Thanks, Mr. Todd."

"You're welcome. You'd better go home and get that schoolwork done. Thanks again for helping out around here."

Tony waved and headed out the door. Nicole hesitated. "Don't feel obligated to come."

"Are you kidding?" Brent didn't waste the small window of opportunity that presented itself. He leaned in and placed a kiss to her soft cheek. "I get to watch Tony play and hang out with you. Sounds great to me."

She ducked her head, but there was no missing the smile that toyed with the corners of her mouth. "See you tonight, Brent."

"I can't wait."

The rest of the day seemed to drag as he kept watching the clock. With someone stopping by the shelter at the last minute to adopt a cat, Brent didn't get to the skating rink as early as he would've liked to.

Practice was in full swing when he entered the building. It only took a moment to pick Nicole out of the crowd of spectators. She was visiting with two women she was sitting near. Brent took an empty spot next to Nicole.

She brightened. "Hey. You made it."

"I did. That guy finally took both goats and someone else adopted a cat." Brent offered the other women a friendly nod.

"That's great." Nicole motioned to the person beside her. "Have you met Savannah Miller or Alisyn Bennett?"

"I don't think so." Brent introduced himself and shook the women's hands. "Do you both have sons on the team?"

The ladies chuckled and Savannah shook her head. "We're both just the transportation." She pointed to one of the boys playing his heart out on the rink. "I've been bringing my nephew, Kyle, in for practice this year."

Alisyn waved to a boy Brent recognized from the work day at the rescue center. "And I bring Cooper. I'm the Rockford's nanny so I'm almost always here." A man walked up, gave Alisyn a smile, and sat down next to her. "This is Shane. He's Cooper's older brother and in town for a few more days."

They all visited and watched the boys play for a while.

Brent shifted on the metal bench to look at Nicole. "Tony is quite an effective defenseman."

Nicole smiled at the compliment. "He's a wall out there. When he first played, he was shorter than anyone else. The other players didn't expect him to stand his ground. Now he's taller than most of the other boys."

Brent watched the scrimmage for a bit. What he wanted to do was reach for Nicole's hand or drape his arm around her shoulder. Instead, he leaned in close enough for his upper arm to rest against hers. "I'm happy to stick around and help you guys clean up after practice."

"That would be great. Thank you."

"You're welcome." It was worth it if it meant getting to spend more time with her.

~

Nicole found being near Brent during Tony's hockey practice a challenge. On one hand, she'd been thrilled to see him come into the building. Her pulse had thrummed in her ears when he sat next to her. On the other hand, it was impossible to focus on anything her other friends were saying when all she could think about was the way Brent's aftershave smelled or how his arm kept brushing hers. How was she supposed to keep an emotional distance when all she wanted to do was slide closer to him? Nicole oscillated between enjoying his presence and knowing she should probably get up and mingle with the other parents. Just to put some space between herself and Brent.

That's what she ought to do, but it didn't make it easy. Especially when Brent managed to make her laugh. A lot. She couldn't remember the last time she'd had that much fun at a practice. Probably not a good thing.

Before she knew it, Jim had spoken to the boys, and they were getting ready to go home with their parents. Tony skated up to them, hair wet with sweat and plastered to his forehead. "Mr. Todd! I knew you'd come. Did you see me block Wade earlier?"

"I did. Fantastic job." Brent extended a hand and exchanged a knuckle bump with Tony. "You guys are looking great. Excited about your next game?"

"Oh, yeah." Someone called his name and Tony waved at Cooper. "I'll be back in a minute."

Nicole and Brent spent the next ten minutes talking to people and saying goodbye as the rink cleared out. Tony took his skates off, and when it was finally just the three of them, they started cleaning the place up.

Nicole did a quick tour of the restrooms. When she returned, she found both guys out on the rink in their shoes with hockey sticks. The two scrimmaged against each other, racing from one end of the rink to the other. Between the mock tough-guy expressions and the good-natured pushing, it was clear they were both having a blast.

She leaned against a wall and watched. She couldn't remember the last time Tony had this much guy attention. It was clear he was eating it up. Her son hadn't stopped talking about Brent for weeks.

He'd been excited all afternoon at the prospect of Brent coming to practice. She took pity on him and cut science a little short because he wasn't focusing, anyway. Tony sure was taken with Brent. She couldn't blame him — she had to admit that she was, too. But what would Tony have done if Brent hadn't shown up tonight?

Brent used to be a regular at the rink until he'd disappeared. Sure, he'd had good reasons. But what if things got super busy, and it happened again? Except, this time it would be different. Tony would be devastated to lose his new best friend.

The good mood that had lifted her spirits turned into worry. It settled over her like a blanket of dew on a cool morning, dampening her mood. A chill jolted up her spine, and she crossed her arms in front of her with a frown.

She'd spent years protecting Tony from that kind of disappointment. He'd had to deal with too much of it in his young life.

The guys finished their scrimmage and put the equipment away. Still laughing, they rejoined her. Brent must have sensed something changed because his eyes narrowed in concern. Nicole ignored it and used one hand to mess up Tony's hair. "Ready to go home? You need to get a shower and something to eat."

"I'm starving." He smoothed his hair back down good-naturedly.

The three of them left the rink, and Nicole locked the place up behind them.

Brent met her eyes over the top of Tony's head. "Can I call you later?"

Trying her best to keep her expression neutral, she nodded.

Brent hesitated but finally shook Tony's hand. "Great job tonight. Have a good rest of your week. I guess I'll see you on Tuesday?" He turned to Nicole. "I'll talk to you soon."

"Thanks for coming, Brent. It meant a lot to Tony." She mustered what she hoped was a normal smile. "Good night."

Her decision to keep distance between herself and Brent was sound. How come she didn't feel any better?

Chapter Eight

Something had changed, though Brent wasn't sure what it was. He left the skating rink with a heavy heart. There was no way he was waiting until Tuesday to decipher what was going on. He gave it an hour, hoping that was long enough for Nicole and Tony to get home and settled before calling her.

She answered on the second ring. "Hey."

"You guys make it home okay?"

"Yeah. Tony's on his second bowl of cereal then he's going to bed. Tonight wore him out."

"I'll bet." Brent had gone over several conversations in his head over the last hour. But even now, with her on the line, what was he supposed to say? He finally opted for a more direct approach. "I was wondering if you and Tony would like to go somewhere Saturday evening. Maybe see that new Marvel movie in the theater." He held his breath as he waited for her response.

"Brent…"

"It'll be fun. Tony mentioned how much he liked those movies. Did you guys see it yet?" As if prolonging her opportunity to speak would change what she was about to say.

"This isn't a good idea."

There it was. Her words hit him like a punch to the gut. "I've thought about you a lot. For years. And I should've done something about it before now. I care about you, and I'd like to continue spending time with you." His stomach tightened in response to her silence. "What is it, Nicole?"

"Look, I don't know how much you know about my life. But Tony's father left him — left us — when Tony was a baby. By the time Tony was six, I'd accepted that it needs to be the two of us. I've done it on my own, and I'm okay with that. I always have been." She paused. "I've done everything in my power to make sure Tony never has to face that kind of rejection again. Because he shouldn't have to."

He wished they were speaking in person so she could see the sincerity in his eyes. Then she'd know just how serious he was about what he planned to say. "I wouldn't do that. To you or Tony. I'd like to think you know me well enough to believe that."

"I'm not sure I can risk that with anyone. I have to put Tony's needs first."

"So, you'd rather push people away and be alone. To protect Tony?" Brent didn't believe for a moment that was the only reason. "Or to protect yourself?" Her silence told him he'd hit the nail on the head.

"I'm not alone. Tony and I: We have each other." Her voice sounded strained. "It's better if I avoid any complications."

MELANIE D. SNITKER

Brent flinched when her words stung like a slap to the face. Hadn't he shown her that he accepted Tony? Enjoyed being around him? "If you could give this a chance…"

"I can't."

Those two words deflated the balloon of hope Brent had been grasping. Maybe calling her hadn't been a good idea. If he'd brought it up to her in person, he could've convinced her how serious he was about both her and Tony.

"Brent?"

"Yeah."

"I'm sorry."

Yeah, so was he.

The phone call ended, and Brent resisted the urge to send his phone flying at the wall in frustration. He pictured it in pieces on the floor, mirroring his hope of a future with Nicole and Tony, and his heart ached.

~

On the outside, Brent's weekend was relatively quiet. He finished painting the trim on the house when weather allowed and went over the extensive list for the festival. On Sunday, he even relaxed and finished a dystopian book he'd been reading by AJ Powers the last couple of weeks.

But no matter how busy he kept himself, it didn't stop him from replaying their conversation repeatedly in his mind. He kept searching for things he could've said to change her response. It'd made it nearly impossible to focus on anything else.

In the end, though, he realized that he'd done everything in his power. If she wouldn't give him the chance to prove how felt... The ball wasn't in his corner, as much as he wished it were.

He found his heart couldn't wait to see them on Tuesday, while his mind dreaded how difficult it could be to work with her after everything that'd transpired at the end of last week.

If it was a distraction he needed, Monday more than obliged. Hattie, who always helped organize the festival, tripped on some stairs and broke her leg. Her daughter came from Salem to pick Hattie up and take her home for a few weeks while she recovered.

While Brent was incredibly sorry for her and the pain she was going through, it also left him scrambling to pick up where poor Hattie left off. He'd have to remember to send her flowers and thank her for all she did – she had no idea how invaluable she'd been.

Now he was making phone calls and taking bites of his sandwich in between. Even Stormy had sensed he needed the space and wasn't begging for a bite of his lunch.

By the time Tuesday rolled around, his to-do list had only grown. A call first thing in the morning revealed a mix-up with the booths and the way they were set up at the town square. As soon as help arrived for the day, Brent needed to go over there and get it worked out in person.

The proceeds from the festival were going to play a huge role in whether the rescue center remained open through next year. Its success now rested largely on his ability to keep things under control in Hattie's absence. Brent was trying hard not to let that extra responsibility weigh his spirits down.

Walt walked in with a wave. "Good morning, Mr. Todd."

Brent breathed a sigh of relief. "Hey, Walt. How are you today?"

Walt frowned. "Actually, I needed to talk to you about something. With this being my last year at the university and all, things are getting hectic. I can't seem to catch a breath." He paused, and Brent steeled himself for what he knew coming. "I'm going to give my two-week's notice. You know I'd stay if I could, but…"

"Don't worry about it, Walt. You've been a huge help, and we couldn't have made it this far without you." Brent stuck his hand out. "I get it. Your classes need to be your priority. And I appreciate the two weeks to get everything straightened out."

Walt let out a shaky laugh and shook Brent's hand. "No problem. Thanks for understanding."

"Of course." Brent's mind went into overdrive as Walt got to work. He'd been worried he might not have the money to keep Walt on after the end of the year. He should be relieved. But he also just lost one of his best helpers, and that was going to hurt.

More than ever, he relied on the festival being successful. He not only needed it to bring in funds for the rescue center, but to find a record number of homes for the animals waiting as well. So much for not letting the pressure get to him.

What if, even after everything people did Saturday to help Finding Forever, he had to close the center? Mr. Rice probably would've understood, but it felt like failure nonetheless.

He tried to shrug off the worry and doubts. They still had the festival. Claire was coming to help and take a few of the critters back with her, too, if necessary.

There was a lot more hope for Finding Forever than there had been a couple of weeks ago. And it was almost all thanks to a cute little redhead who'd captured his heart. He thought about their kiss for the hundredth time. So much for being busy enough to keep their phone conversation from haunting him.

Speaking of Nicole. The door chime sounded as she and Tony came inside.

He swallowed past the lump in his throat and forced a casual smile. "Hey, you two. I've got to run over to the square and sort out some problems we're having with the booths. Nicole, would you mind keeping an eye on the farmhouse? With the festival coming up, not many people will be by. And you have my cell number if something comes up and you need me to come back for an adoption."

Nicole's eyes widened. "No problem. Anything else we can do?" She looked uncertain as she fiddled with the hem of her shirt.

Brent took some satisfaction in seeing he wasn't the only one affected by the weird situation between them. "No, it'll just be a huge relief knowing you're here helping Walt keep an eye on the place. I'll be back before one." He ignored the twinge of pain in his heart as he left.

He'd gone back and forth between looking forward to seeing them and dreading the changes their conversation was sure to have on their friendship. He wished he didn't have to leave the shelter immediately, yet he wasn't sure he could handle being around her for hours with things the way they were. But when he got to the town square, he was glad he'd gone there in person. With the help of several volunteers, they finally got everything figured out. The large park area in the center of town was bordered by streets on all four sides of it. Usually, most of the booths were kept on one side of the street, but there were more entries than ever before. A great problem to have, but it meant going through all the right city channels to have three streets blocked off.

That meant they could use white paint to denote where the booths would set up along the border of the park.

Brent stood in the gazebo and peered out over the area. There was still a lot of work to do, but there was no doubt about it: This festival would dwarf all the others before it.

~

Nicole found the week full of mixed emotions. For one, she hardly saw Brent. She should be glad. There was no time for the awkwardness she was sure would exist. After talking on the phone a few days ago, she'd been determined to keep some distance between them this last week of volunteering. But with his crazy schedule, she didn't even have to worry about that. Where there should've been relief, disappointment reigned. The familiar tendrils of loneliness pushed their way in.

On top of that, Tony seemed more and more depressed the closer they got to the festival. He said he was fine, but based on the time he spent with Costello, she was certain he was dreading having to say goodbye to the giant dog. The knowledge hurt Nicole's heart because, if she had any way to keep Costello, she'd let Tony take him home. She'd grown attached to the guy herself and often checked on him to see how his leg was doing. Not that she'd admit it.

Brent was right. They had few visitors all week with everyone in town getting ready for the festival. Apparently, most of the issues had been worked out, and they'd be ready when the festival started at nine Saturday morning. She and Tony had promised to help at the adoption tent, for which Brent seemed thankful.

Nicole was in with the cats when Brent returned from running errands on Thursday. "Everything on track for Saturday?"

"Yep, I think we're a go. My cousin, Claire, will get here sometime this evening. She'll help me set up the adoption tent first thing tomorrow and transfer the animals to the festival on Saturday morning."

Without meaning to, Nicole's gaze went to Callie. She remained hunched in the back of her crate, peering at them from the darkness. "What do you need Tony and I to do?"

"If you guys could be at the tent at eight thirty, we'll be ready for when everyone comes by. Then stay as late as you want, but don't feel obligated to work all day. Between the three of us, Claire, Walt, and Stacie, and some other people who have volunteered, we'll have the tent covered." Brent rubbed the back of his neck before letting his hand fall to his side. "I can't thank you and Tony enough for all you've done the last few weeks."

What neither of them were saying weighed heavy in the air. Nicole shuffled her feet a little and clasped her hands together behind her back. "We're happy we could help."

Brent glanced at the door to the hallway and stepped closer to Nicole. "I'll miss you. Both of you."

He reached out and held her elbow in his hand. "I wish you'd reconsider. I want to keep seeing you after this weekend."

There was no missing his intention. He was watching her, his emotions on the surface. She didn't know what to say. Her heart begged her to shout yes. But what if Tony was uncomfortable with the idea of her dating Brent? She couldn't do it. Not right now. She swallowed and blinked back the tears. "Brent, I..." Her voice faltered.

Disappointment flashed across his face before he stood straighter and brought his hand back to his side. "If Tony has decided which dog he'd like, let me know, and I can be sure to keep it here."

Nicole nodded.

Brent pointed to the calico. "It still amazes me she won't come out. She waits in that cage, convinced it's the safest place for her to be." His voice sounded sad. "She'd rather hide for an indefinite amount of time than see what might happen if she took a chance." His gaze went back to Nicole's. "I need to check on the farm animals. I'll see you on Saturday." With a tight smile, Brent turned and left the room.

Nicole let out a shaky breath and crouched down in front of Callie's crate. "Is that true, girl? Are you afraid to take a chance? Would you rather sit in the back of your crate forever? If you came out, you might find someone to adopt you. You could have the forever family you deserve."

Her voice caught. What if that's exactly what Nicole was doing? Was she using Tony as her excuse to keep her heart buried? Would she rather hang back and live her life the way she always had because she was afraid to take a chance?

Goosebumps peppered her skin, and she held herself around the middle. Was it possible to have the happy family she'd always dreamed of?

~

Nicole was determined to talk to Tony about Brent tonight. But first, she wanted to ask him if he'd decided which dog he wanted to adopt. She made them both a mug of hot chocolate and waited for him on the living room couch.

Tony walked in, his brown hair still damp from his shower, and paused warily. "Uh oh."

She laughed. "No lecture or anything like that. Can't a mom make her son some hot chocolate?" She patted the couch to show him she wanted him to sit down.

Tony appeared amused. "You kidding? Anytime." He did as she suggested and reached for the mug closest to him. "But something tells me there's more going on." He sipped his hot chocolate and then blew on the liquid a little.

The boy was smart. "I was wondering if you'd decided which dog you'd like to adopt after the festival."

His smile disappeared, and he shrugged. "I'll wait to see which dogs are left."

"Because you want Costello."

He shrugged again, and Nicole's heart went out to him. "You know there's a good chance Costello won't be adopted. If that happens, maybe we could keep volunteering once a week. That way, you can see him regularly."

Tony looked a little more hopeful. "Yeah. That would be good." He paused for a moment, staring into his drink. "Do you think Mr. Todd will send Costello with his cousin?"

Nicole chuckled. "I doubt it. His cousin is driving. I can't imagine there'll be enough room in her car for Costello." She laughed, glad to see Tony's eyes light up as he joined her.

"You're probably right." He took another drink. "Can we really keep volunteering?"

"Absolutely." She hadn't even bothered taking a sip of her hot chocolate yet. Truthfully, she was way too nervous. "What do you think of Brent?"

"He's awesome! It'd be great to own a place like Finding Forever and help animals like he does." He cupped his mug with both hands. "All the guys on the team think it's great how Brent let us paint and help with stuff."

Nicole wanted to smile but was too busy weighing her next words. "So, you wouldn't mind if he was around more often?" She watched as Tony's eyes slowly widened with realization.

He tossed a look her way that landed somewhere between wary and curious. "What do you mean?"

She'd rehearsed all of this in her head a dozen times since they were at the shelter that afternoon. "I like Brent a lot. But I would never even consider dating him unless you were one hundred percent okay with it." Her voice caught, and she took a moment to focus.

Tony set his mug back down on the coffee table with a clunk. "Mom…"

"If it makes you uncomfortable, I just want you to be honest and tell me…"

"Mom!"

Nicole's eyebrows lifted, and she stopped.

Tony gave her a smile. "It's okay."

"What is?"

"If you and Brent date. He's a good guy. You deserve to be happy."

Nicole shook her head. When had her little boy grown up this much? Her eyes misted over, and she blinked rapidly to bring Tony's face back into focus. "Are you sure?" The question came out as more of a whisper.

"Yeah." Tony reached over and patted her arm. "I'm sure. Besides, if he does anything to hurt you, me and the whole team will go rough him up a little."

Nicole burst out laughing at that. "You're something else, kiddo. You know that? I'm proud of you." She pulled Tony into a tight hug.

"Thanks, Mom." Tony's voice was muffled against her shoulder. "I can't breathe."

She released him and they both laughed.

Nicole's hope soared. Everything she'd worried about suddenly seemed less pressing. She longed to talk to Brent tonight, but it was late. Plus, Claire was supposed to be at the rescue center first thing tomorrow morning, and Nicole didn't want to interrupt their reunion. She'd waited this long, she could wait another day and see if she had the chance to talk to him after the festival.

She only prayed it wouldn't be too late.

Chapter Nine

Brent had gone into the festival hoping the record number of booths would equal an increase in attendees. Any expectations he had were blown away.

When Nicole and Tony got there, he had just enough time to introduce them to Claire before three people came in to browse the animals. It never slowed down much. By noon, two of the cats, both guinea pigs, several dogs, and two of the ferrets had all been adopted.

The couple Brent had been helping left with their new pet. Grateful for a moment to breathe, he turned and watched as Nicole helped an older lady browse the cats. When she stopped in front of the calico, Nicole looked stricken. Biting back a smile, he joined them.

"I'm sorry, but I believe this one is already adopted." He waited for Nicole to lift her blue eyes to his. "Isn't that right?"

She glanced from him to the crate. "Yes, that's right."

The older lady gave a little nod. "That's good, that's good. What about this little black one over here?"

Nicole flashed Brent a smile and whispered, "Thank you," before answering the other lady's questions.

Brent happily wrote "Adopted" on a card and taped it to the calico's crate. He'd watched Nicole become more and more attached to the cat over the last three weeks and knew it would be hard for her to say goodbye. Not to mention, she seemed to be the only one who could connect with the cat.

Claire walked up and nodded at the largest kennel where Costello was waiting. The poor guy looked pathetic with his bandaged leg and the cone of shame still secured around his neck. But there was Tony, always nearby. "Please don't make me take that behemoth to New York."

Brent tipped his head back and laughed. "I think he's capable of pulling your car all the way there." He watched as Tony absently petted the dog's head. Costello was lying on the ground with his body as close to the side of the kennel as he could get it. "Besides, I think someone would be sad to see him go." He checked the time. "Why don't you go grab something to eat?"

Claire pushed some of her dark brown hair away from her face. "Want me to bring anything back for you?"

"A couple of chicken skewers would be great. Thanks."

"You got it, cuz. I won't take too long." Claire bent to scratch the ears of a French bulldog, waved, and disappeared into the crowd of shoppers.

Someone came up behind Brent. He knew, before he turned, that it was Nicole. "Hey, you."

"Your cousin seems nice. It's obvious you two get along well."

"We do. I wish we had the opportunity to see each other more often." He paused. "I'm glad you kept the calico."

"Me, too. Thanks for stepping in there like that." She stopped at his side.

"What was the deciding factor?"

"Something you said. I thought Callie and I could help each other let go of the past so we can move toward new possibilities." She leaned over and let her arm rest against his.

Brent's heart hammered in his chest. What exactly did she mean? Was he reading too much into it? He shifted to see her. "Nicole, I…"

Marshall, one of his volunteers, jogged up to them. "Hey, Brent. I need to get all the paperwork for Chance."

Brent studied Nicole's face, trying to decipher the meaning behind her previous words. It'd have to wait. He turned to Marshall and his brows rose. He'd hesitated to bring the horse to the festival because the poor guy was so skittish around men. "Who's interested in him?"

"Katie Mackall." Marshall grinned.

"Nice." Katie was one of the few people Brent thought could reach Chance and make a difference in the horse's life. "Make sure you tell Katie about his history."

"Will do, boss."

Brent took one more peek at Nicole before leading Marshall to the table and the files he kept on each of the animals.

~

Nicole bit into the pumpkin donut and closed her eyes in bliss. She looked forward to the pastries every year. It was after one in the afternoon, and her stomach had been growling for a while. Tony polished off his donut and was starting on a second one.

Brent insisted they take a break to walk around for a few minutes and get something for lunch. It'd taken a lot for Nicole to drag Tony away from Costello. The boy was eating as fast as possible so he could get back. They'd found a spot on the grass under a tree where they rested their feet for a few minutes.

Nicole pointed across the way to where several people were painting characters on children's cheeks and hands. "You used to love having your face painted. Do you remember?"

He nodded. "Yeah. I think my favorite was the time I had an entire Batman mask painted. That was awesome." He chortled and pointed two booths down. "Check it out."

Under the canopy, an Australian Shepherd stood with her front legs on a table. Her tail wagged, and her whole body moved back and forth along with it. The sign above her read, "Pet Kissing Booth." The next person in line handed over some money and then leaned forward, letting the dog lick him on the face.

Nicole and Tony laughed hard enough, it made it almost impossible to finish their food. The funniest part was that the dog never seemed to tire. If too much time passed between customers, she'd lick the air as if she were enticing the people walking by.

"What a brilliant idea." Nicole swallowed her last bite and stood up, brushing any bits of grass that might remain off her pants.

"Can you imagine Costello doing that?" Tony was ready to get back to the adoption tent. He even took her trash and threw it away for her. "What time is it?"

Nicole checked her phone. "A few minutes after two."

"Less than four hours to go."

They walked that way, and Tony seemed relieved to find Costello was waiting for him, tail wagging.

Brent was organizing some of the paperwork at the folding table in the center. Nicole approached him. "How're we doing?"

"Over half the animals have found homes, including the horse." He grinned in triumph. "There's been some interest in a few others, but I haven't heard from those people yet. Did you get something to eat?"

"I did."

"Good." Brent crossed his arms and sat on the edge of the table. "If things calm down, could I convince you to go on a hayride with me?"

Nicole raked strands of hair with one hand and smiled. "I think that can be arranged."

He nodded once, a grin on his face as his gaze locked with hers. Her heart fluttered in her chest but she couldn't look away. All the noise around them seemed to fade until the sound of her own blood rushing filled her ears.

She moved to sit on the edge of the table with him, painfully aware of how close they were. He covered her hand with his and this time, the last thing she wanted to do was move away.

But it wasn't long before someone else came along, and Brent was off saving the world one pet at a time.

~

"Are you sure you don't want to come with us?" Nicole asked her son about forty minutes before the end of the festival.

"I'm sure, Mom. Go ahead." Tony gave her a subtle wink. "I'll stay and keep Costello company."

Claire nodded. "I'll keep an eye on everything. Besides, things have slowed down."

Nicole met Brent's eyes. "Okay, then. I guess we can go."

It was about time. Ever since they'd agreed to go on a hayride, it was all he thought about. As they walked away from the adoption tent, their hands found each other. He ran his thumb over hers.

What she'd said earlier had been a little cryptic. He wanted the chance to ask her exactly what she meant by it. Because he was certain he knew what he wanted.

They got in line just as the red wagon full of hay bales approached, pulled by two large Belgian draft horses. Blayne Grundy was driving the wagon and when he noticed Brent, he raised a hand in greeting.

Enough people had gone home for the evening to make it possible for Brent and Nicole to get an entire bale to themselves. Brent braced a hand on the prickly hay behind Nicole, enjoying the way she was leaning against his shoulder. "I don't know about you, but my feet are killing me."

Nicole nodded, her hair brushing his cheek. "Mine, too. But we did well. I'm not even sure there'll be any animals left for Claire to take back to New York."

Brent had been thinking about that all day. If he had a fraction of the animals to feed for the next month or more, he might be able to afford to build the other outdoor kennel. Especially after getting updates on the proceeds from the festival thus far. There was no doubt this would be the most profitable year yet.

He leaned a little closer to her and spoke just loud enough for her to hear. "What you said earlier. About the calico. Were you only talking about the cat?"

"Not entirely." She turned her head slightly to look at him. "I think Callie and I have a lot in common. I've spent too many years trying to keep my heart from breaking again, backing myself up into a corner."

"And now?" He held his breath as the wagon carried them down the street.

"Now I'm wondering what I might lose if I don't take a chance and explore the possibilities."

Brent lifted his arm and placed it around her shoulders, relishing the feel of holding her close. "I'm glad. Because I know I'd miss out on something pretty special with a beautiful lady."

She shifted slightly, her face merely inches away. Without hesitation, he captured her lips with his, not caring who was around to see it. She melted in his embrace, and that was all he needed to draw her closer.

Moments later, they pulled apart, and she rested her head against his shoulder. "You're amazing, you know that?"

Brent placed a kiss to her forehead. "Right back at you."

The hayride came full circle and stopped. Brent helped Nicole down before lacing his fingers with hers. They thanked Blayne for the ride and meandered their way across the grass.

Nicole pointed to one of the nearby booths. "Did you see the blown glass? There was an article about the owner, I think her name's Brooke, in the newspaper. She makes it all by hand."

"Did you want to stop and look?" The evening sun lit up the colorful glass items and made them sparkle.

"No, it looks like she's about ready to close up shop. She has a store in town, I'll swing by next week. I always buy my mom a new Christmas ornament. I'll bet Brooke will have something unique I can send her this year."

The continued their walk. Up ahead, under the tent, Costello still sat with Tony nearby.

Nicole shook her head. "I'm going to end up with that dog, aren't I?"

Brent laughed. "I'm not sure how you'll get around it." He lifted her hand and placed a kiss against her knuckles. "But I may have a plan."

They stopped walking, and Nicole turned to him. "Really?"

He nodded. "Walt gave his two-week notice. What if you took his job and came to work at Finding Forever? We can keep Costello there at the shelter, and Tony can see him and play with him every day."

"Are you serious?"

The hope in her eyes had him smiling. He put his arms around her and pulled her close. "I couldn't be more serious. About anyone."

"It sounds perfect."

Epilogue
Two Months Later

Nicole absently pushed the bench swing with the toe of her shoe. She laughed as Tony raced across the yard with Costello loping beside him. Now that the dog's cast was off, and he was no longer condemned to a life with his head in a cone, he'd enjoyed his never-ending energy. And Tony never seemed to tire of playing with him.

The swing jerked as Brent joined her and then settled back into its even rhythm. He put an arm around her. "Those two are quite the pair, aren't they?"

"They sure are." Nicole rested her head against his shoulder, only to lift it a moment later. "By the way, you let me adopt a defective cat."

His eyebrows rose. "Oh?"

"Tony opened the door to take the trash out last night, and a sparrow flew into the house. It took twenty minutes to shoo it back outside. And what did Callie do the entire time?"

Brent was chuckling. "I couldn't even guess."

"She hid under the coffee table as if that little bird would dive-bomb and kill her."

They were both laughing now.

"You could always adopt another one."

She shook her head. "Nope, one cat is enough for that little house."

He reached for her left hand and held it gently in his. He ran his thumb over the shiny engagement ring on her finger. "But once we're married and you move into the farmhouse with me?"

Peace unlike anything Nicole had ever known settled over her heart. "That's different. Maybe Stormy can teach Callie a thing or two."

"Maybe so." Brent nuzzled her cheek. "I love you, Nicole."

"I love you, too."

Tony ran past and then doubled back, breathing hard. "Mom, can we get pizza tonight?"

Nicole nodded. "I think we can arrange that."

Costello ran to Tony's side but instead of stopping, he put his front paws on the swing between Brent and Nicole, tongue hanging out in what resembled a grin.

They all laughed as Brent struggled to get Costello's feet back on the ground.

Tony put an arm around the dog's neck. "I'll be glad when you get married. I'm looking forward to never having to leave Costello again." Without another word, he raced off, the dog on his heels.

Brent winked at Nicole. "I can't wait to marry you, either. For a lot of reasons." He kissed her until they were both breathless.

Nicole curled into his side, more content than she ever thought she'd be. After everything they'd been through, she finally had the forever family she'd always dreamed of.

A Note from the Author

Thank you for reading *Finding Forever in Romance*. This story was a lot of fun to write, and it's been a pleasure to work with the other authors in this autumn-themed collection. When we first started creating the town of Romance, we had no idea how much this place would mean to all of us. We hope you'll feel the same as you *Fall Into Romance* and get to know the wonderful characters that live there.

There are many details in *Finding Forever in Romance* that are close to my heart. I was homeschooled from the first grade through high school. My husband and I now homeschool both of our children as well. And you wouldn't know it to look at me, but I played roller hockey in high school and college. I still enjoy going inline skating.

I also got inspiration for Mr. Rice's lollipop tree from my grandpa. One time, when my brothers and I were very young, Grandpa hung a strip of lollipops on a tree and told us that it was a lollipop tree. My youngest brother, especially, was fascinated with the concept.

Adopting animals in need of homes is another matter that's very important to me. Nearly every pet we've had has been a rescue animal of one kind or another. Whether the dog landed on our front porch, we saw it running down the side of the highway, or we rescued it from the humane society, each one left a permanent pawprint on our hearts. If you have room in your home for a pet, I encourage you to consider adopting one from your local animal rescue or shelter.

If you enjoyed *Finding Forever in Romance*, would you please consider leaving a review? Doing so would help other readers find books they might enjoy. Thank you!

If you enjoyed *Finding Forever In Romance*, please be sure to read the rest of the books in the **Fall Into Romance** collection.

Finding Forever in Romance by Melanie D. Snitker - Brent's hands are so full he doesn't realize his heart is empty. But how can he convince Nicole to trust him and give them all a chance at the forever family they deserve?

Lost in Romance by Stacy Claflin - Work is Alisyn's life. Everything is perfect until the day her boss's son comes to town and takes her breath away. Will she risk it all for love?

At Second Glance by Raine English - Can an ornery French bulldog help a mismatched couple find love?

Blown Into Romance by Shanna Hatfield - Free spirit Brooke Roberts blows into Romance like an autumn storm, unprepared to fall for the handsome rancher who gives her a reason to stay.

Wired for Romance by Franky A. Brown - Electrician Josh Chadwick can rewire his new client's house, but he can't do a thing about the electricity sparking between them.

Restoring Romance by Tamie Dearen - She's a big city chef who likes cats. He's a small town mayor who restores antiques. But even with feline allergies at play, true love is nothing to sneeze at.

Finding Dori by J.J. DiBenedetto - She's a loud, pushy New Yorker who drives him crazy. He almost ran her over with his truck. Of course they're perfect for each other…

Katie's Chance for Romance by Jessica L. Elliott - Five years ago she pushed him out of her life, but she couldn't force him from her heart.

Chasing Romance by Liwen Y. Ho - When pop sensation Chase Lockhart wants more than a room at Izzy Sutton's Bed and Breakfast, she must decide whether it's worth opening up her heart to him, especially when he's eleven years her junior.

Lessons in Romance by Kit Morgan - A rooster, a tortoise and love, oh my! Now if the humans could just figure out the love part, they might all live happily ever after.

If you've fallen in love with the quirky, fun, charming characters of Romance, be sure to watch for future stories. You can keep up on all the Welcome to Romance news on Facebook here: https://www.facebook.com/welcometoromance/

About the Author

Melanie D. Snitker has enjoyed writing fiction for as long as she can remember. She started out writing episodes of cartoon shows that she wanted to see as a child and her love of writing grew from there. She and her husband live in Texas with their two children who keep their lives full of adventure, and two dogs who add a dash of mischief to the family dynamics. In her spare time, Melanie enjoys photography, reading, crochet, baking, archery, target shooting, and hanging out with family and friends.

http://www.melaniedsnitker.com
https://twitter.com/MelanieDSnitker
https://www.facebook.com/melaniedsnitker

Subscribe to Melanie's newsletter and receive a monthly e-mail containing recipes, information about new releases, giveaways, and more! You can find a link to sign up on her website.

Books by Melanie D. Snitker

Calming the Storm
(A Marriage of Convenience)

Love's Compass Series:
Finding Peace
Finding Hope
Finding Courage
Finding Faith
Finding Joy

Life Unexpected Series:
Safe In His Arms
Someone to Trust

Made in United States
North Haven, CT
21 March 2024

50276846R00068